THE SILENT VARIABLE

DHRUV TRIPATHI

Contents

Acknowledgements

"Thank you, Dad, for always being my strength and my guide."

CHAPTER I

SOL 17

The martial dust clung to everything, like it knew they didn't belong.

The lander touched down with a metallic groan, and for a heartbeat, no one spoke. Sixteen people, frozen in awe and fear inside a steel shell, breathing recycled air for the first of what would be thousands of days.

Commander Olivia Sinclair was the first to unclip. Her voice crackled over the intercom.

" This is Commander Sinclair. Touchdown confirmed. Mars One is live."

There was no cheering. Only silence.

Not reverent. Not stunned. Just... silence. Like the planet itself was listening.

They called the landing site ALETHEIA BASE , named after the Greek word for "truth" . ironically.

The team disembarked in pairs, suited sealed tight, boots crunching into virgin regolith. The wind howled like a ghost, thin and high and sharp. Mars was a dead world, but somehow it felt like it had teeth .

Dr. Leon Voss was last out. He moved slowly, deliberately, already scanning soil samples, muttering into his recorder. He seemed more excited by microbial life than the fact they were the first humans on another planet.

Others had different reactions.

Lieutenant Ava Marquez, head of security, kept her hand near her sidearm—standard-issue, "for emergencies." She didn't like silence, and Mars had plenty of it.

Engineer Jonas Beltran cracked a joke about being the first to take a dump on the red planet. No one laughed.

Dr. Kira Lang, psychologist, kept watching the others—analyzing, cataloging. She wasn't here to observe Mars. She was here to observe them.

And in the middle of it all, stood Olivia. Watching her team. Watching the planet.

They all believed they were alone.

By Sol 07, the first signs of tension began to show.

Jonas argued with Ava over power prioritization. The hydroponics system tripped a false alarm and filled half the base with ammonia vapor. Voss requested a full isolation lab—something about "sensitive biomatter readings" in the lower valley.Olivia denied the request.

He didn't argue. He just stared at her, silent, as if trying to decide something.

By Sol 13, Kira began logging dreams.

Not hers. Everyone else's.

Recurring dreams. Shared imagery. Red landscapes covered in black symbols. A man standing outside the dome, waving. Calling.

"I know it's probably psychological," Kira told Olivia. "Dream contamination. Collective stress response. But the symbols...they match old carvings found in Antarctic rocks. Prehistoric ones."

Olivia dismissed it. "Dreams don't matter. Reality does."

Kira hadn't looked convinced.

Mars was supposed to be quiet.

Predictable. Sterile.

Commander Olivia Sinclair had counted on that.

She sat at her console in the main habitat , recording the daily systems report - oxygen levels ,water reclamation efficiency , core temperature - all within normal parameters. Her voice was calm, steady, the way it always was.

Sol 17. No anomalies. Hydroponics report shows an 8% increase in nutrient absorption. Still no communication from Earth - assumed solar interference continues.

Then it happened.

A sound that didn't belong.

Not static . Not equipment failure.

A scream.

High pitched, ragged, human. Male.

And close.

Olivia froze mid- sentence . For a split second,she thought it might've come from the comm system. Then she realized it was coming from inside the base.

She bolted up, already shouting.

" Habitat C! Who's in Habitat C"?

The response crackled back after a delay. It was muffled, panicked.

" I–I think it's Voss! I'm in the D block – I heard it too, Olivia. What the hell is going on?"

Dr. Leon Voss. The biologist. Quiet , meticulous, too intelligent for his own good. He'd spent the last 48 hours running DNA samples on possible Martian extremophiles. He wasn't supposed to be anywhere near Habitat C.

Olivia grabbed her helmet from the rack and sprinted toward the sealed corridor .The emergency lights had begun to flash– a dull red pulse that cast long shadows down the metal hallway.

When she reached the door to Habita C, it was already ajar. That shouldn't have been possible. All internal hatches were pressure – sealed.

Locked. Controlled.

Inside, the lights flickered.

And on the floor, twisted unnaturally beneath the workbench, was Leon Voss.

At first glance, he looked like he'd been mauled blood pooled around his chest, soaking into the grated floor. But when Olivia got closer, she realized the worst part wasn't the torn suit or shattered helmet.

It was his face.

His eyes were gone. Not gouged out–but cleanly, surgically removed. As if plucked.

And smeared across the white polymer wall, written in what could only be his blood, was a single word:

"HOME"

Olivia backed away slowly, barely breathing, her visor fogging up from the heat of her panic. Behind her, one of the engineers– jonas–entered the room and froze in the doorway.

"Holy sh–" he started, but couldn't finish.

No one spoke.

No one moved.

Even on a dead planet, silence could scream.

CHAPTER II

The Fallout

Olivia sealed off Habitat C. Quarantine protocols. No one argued.

The crew gathered in the central dome, their faces lit by the sterile glow of overhead LEDs. No one sat. No one looked each other in the eye. It seemed like all of them had something to hide or was it just the shock.

Their voices were low, clipped, like they were afraid of being overheard.

Even by the walls.

Jonas paced like a caged animal. "He didn't do this to himself. No one rips their own eyes out and bleeds on the wall."

Kira was staring at the word again—HOME. She kept mouthing it silently, trying to understand it. Her notepad was already full.

"We don't know if it was—intentional," Olivia said, but her voice wavered. "He was under pressure. He'd been isolated for—"

"Don't gaslight us, Commander," Ava snapped. "This wasn't madness. It was a message."

Olivia's throat tightened. "Then who left it?"

The silence returned.

The only thing constant since they have laid their eyes on the planet has been nothing but silence.

They tried to contact Earth.

Jonas manned the comms console, rerouting power from non-essentials. "Signal's outbound, but no acknowledgment. Could be solar interference. Could be equipment failure. Could be... worse."

"Try again," Olivia ordered.

Jonas nodded, but the doubt in his eyes was hard to miss.

Later that night, as Mars rotated into darkness, Ava did a perimeter check and found something she couldn't explain.

Boots prints.

Outside the dome.

But not from their suits. Different tread.

Heavier.

Only one set.

They led out into the dark, stopped about 300 meters away...and vanished.

Olivia didn't sleep. Neither did Kira. or maybe they cannot ...

In her room, the psychologist reviewed footage of Voss's final hours. At 0300 hours, he had walked calmly into Habitat C. He had been humming something—old Earth music. The feed cut out exactly four minutes before he was found.

When it returned, he was already dead.

Someone had scrubbed the internal logs. One who could access it.

No prints. No footprints. No security footage.

But one message had been left behind in the corner of his lab. A note. Scrawled in graphite.

Four words.

"He's already here."

"Who is here" , was it someone from the group or maybe an entirely different entity.

Everyone had questions but no one said a word, there was nothing but silence.

At dinner on sol 17, kira ingests something. Not enough to knock her out– just enough to slow her responses, cloud her thoughts. A sedative, maybe something with hallucinogenic properties.

She begins feeling "off" around 0200 hours.

Notes in her journal:

"Dizziness. Difficulty tracking thoughts. Something is wrong with the lights. Shadows too deep."

Her comm log shows an unfinished recording:

" I think someone is tampering with my....[static]...they're not dreams anymore."

At exactly 03:08, the base security feed cuts out for four minutes.

This is not a system error. It's the second precise blackout, suggesting the killer knows how to exploit or override the system– possibly even using pre-written scripts or remote triggers. The timing mirrors Voss's death, pointing to a ritualistic pattern.

During the blackout, someone enters her quarters. The room is fully soundproofed– Kira had requested privacy for her psychological recordings, using layered insulation and blackout material. A detail that now becomes lethal.

She is barely able to resist.

Kira is manually restrained– tied to her desk chair using a combination of duct tape and twisted cabling. Her legs are broken after she's secured, to fit her body into a controlled posture of helplessness.

The injuries suggest precise anatomical knowledge– femurs snapped at midshaft, with no external lacerations, indicating use of blunt internal force. No signs of panic, no scattered objects. Her motor control was likely suppressed chemically or via trauma to the head.

Her mouth is forced open, jaw locked with a splint or some makeshift tool(missing from the scene, likely removed to erase trace evidence). Surgical thread is looped through the outer flesh of her cheeks and lips, pulling her jaw open while simultaneously sealing it.

This makes her expression one of eternal scream– a grotesque performance. Forensics notes a mild numbing agent was used –possibly to keep her from passing out early.

" She wanted to speak the truth. So her mouth was silenced. Permanently open. Never able to close again."

The killer uses strips of her own dermal layers– carefully flayed from her forearms using a scalpel or heat blade– to write the word "LISTEN" on the wall. The cuts are precise , symmetrical, and slow. This part may have been done before death,while she was still conscious.

If so, it suggests extreme calculated cruelty– the killer may have coerced or forced her to watch this process, including total mental collapse before she bled out.

Olivia nearly vomited. Ava didn't flinch, but her hands trembled at her sides. Jonas just started at the wall, not at the body. Like if he didnt see her, he could pretend it was fake. That this wasn't even happening.

Ava finally whispered, "this...this had to take hours. No one heard anything?"

The walls were thin. They should've heard something. But no one had. Not a single sound.

Her journal was missing. Except one torn page. On it, in neat, methodical handwriting, she had written:

" We're not going mad.

He wants us to think it's madness.

But this is a performance.

Someone is watching."

They ran every forensic scan they had. No unknown prints. No foreign materials. No heat signatures. Whosoever– or whatever– had done this knew how to erase themselves.

Ava demanded they begin searching for hiding spots– subfloor compartments, unused vent tunnels, external storage units.

"Someone's in here with us ," she said. "Has been from the start."

But that doesn't explain the footprints. Or the power blackouts. Or how someone coils stitch a woman's face shut in a silent room and make her use her own skin as ink without waking the others.

Kira lang was the psychologist. The observer. The "watcher". She was documenting dreams, hallucinations, and possible early signs of psychosis in the crew.

She was getting too close to the truth it seemed.

That night, Jonas found something else.

Inside Kira's private audio logs–encrypted but hastily hidden– was a voice.

Not hers.

Male.

Soothing.Calm.

Whispering.

" Sixteen hearts.

Seventeen by the end.

The mouth speaks lies.

But the eyes... the eyes always trays tell the truth."

Jonas shut the file and didn't speak for the rest of the day.

Altheia base had stopped breathing. The recycled air still hummed through vents, oxygen still flowed– but no one breathed like before.

After Kira Lang's death, the basse turned into a silent warren of glances, whispers, and suspicion.

Sixteen had come. Now, two were dead–torn apart, mind and body.

And the killer was among them. Or worse, not.

The Psychological Collapse Begins,

Olivia tried to keep order. On sol 19, she initiated full lockdown protocol. All doors required doubled authorization. Mandatory psych evaluations every 6 hours. Personal logs reviewed. Rooms searched.

But each order felt hollower. She no longer slept, not really. Her journal entries became clipped, fractured:

' I can't see where this ends.

Kira knew something.

I didn't listen."

She began talking to herself aloud– mostly at night. Whispering through the walls to people who weren't there.

Jonas heard her one night, murmuring into a blank screen:

" Tell me what you saw, leon. Please . say it this time ..."

Jonas Beltran was an engineer.

He stopped fixing things, the comms systems stayed down. The thermal generations began to hum too loud. Lights flickered. He didn't care. He'd begun spending hours watching playback of Voss's death. Then Kira's.

Freeze. Rewind. Zoom. frame by frame. Searching for movement. Shadows. Patterns.

He stopped eating . cut his hair off with a utility knife. He pinned kira's final note above his bed:

" We are not going mad. Someone is watching"

Sometimes he whispered back to it:

" I know"

Ava Marquez was the security officer, always a soldier, doubled down.

She armed herself with a rifle at all times. Began surveillance rotations even while off–duty, slept only in 15 minute bursts, back to a wall, weapon resting on her chest.

On sol 20 , she accused one of the botanists–Miquel– of being the killer. She shoved him against the wall during hydroponic duty, screaming:

" You're always quiet. You disappear for hours.

What are you hiding"

When Olivia intervened, Ava backed down–but didn't apologize.

Miquel stopped speaking after that. Literally. He went mute. Didn't even answer the roll call.

The rest of the crew split into two silent fractions.

The believers: they thought someone–or something–was already here. That the mission had been a lie. That Kira's dreams were nothing but warnings.

The realists: they thought someone among the crew had snapped. That isolation had turned one of them into a monster.

But even the realists stopped making eye contact after a while. People began sleeping in shifts. No one wanted to be the only one awake.

Or the only one asleep.

By sol 21, the first reported hallucinations appeared.

Ava reported seeing voss walk past her window–outside–where there was no oxygen and no footprints.

Jonas heard Kira's voice in the comm static.

She was whispering:

"He's behind you. Don't turn around"

And then... one of them went missing.

Miquel.

No note. No trace, his room sealed from the inside. Suit gone. Airlock unused. Sensor showed nothing.

Just gone.

Like he never existed at all.

On the evening of sol 21, the crew gathered in the central dome.

Thirteen remained, no one sat. no one spoke at first.

It was Olivia who finally said it"

" He is haunting us"

Jonas shook his head slowly. " No, he's studying us. Like we're the test. Not the mission."

Ava stared into her rifle scope, not even blinking.

" One of you is lying. I can smell it on you"

Olivia didn't answer.

Because in the back of her mind, a new thought had taken root.

Not who was killing them.

But why hasn't the earth responded yet?

It has been four days

They'd sent the message. The call for help. The emergency signal.

But what if... they never received it?

What if someone else had?

CHAPTER III

The Man From The Earth

Dr. Adrian Park sat in front of the deep space telemetry array, sipping burnt coffee and rubbing his eyes.

The Martian communications relay had been experiencing "expected disruption" for three days. A solar eclipse, they said. Magnetic interference. Nothing unusual.

But it was Day 3. And nothing was ever this quiet.

The Intercepted Transmission

At 03:41 UTC, a data packet arrived.

Encrypted. Flagged. Buried in the backchannel.

It wasn't from the main relay.

It was from an unauthorized uplink, routed through an ancient lunar satellite decommissioned over twenty years ago.

Park opened it anyway.

Static. Then a woman's voice—faint, ragged. Familiar.

"This is Dr. Kira Lang... Aletheia Base... there's been a murder. We need... help.

He's not one of us.

He's not from Earth—he's not—"

Then silence. A burst of data followed—a compressed log of atmospheric pressure anomalies, security system loops, vitals spikes. A wall of corrupted code.

Park froze. That voice—it had been marked deceased two sols ago.

He reported it. Of course he did. Straight to Command.

But instead of mobilizing a crisis response, he was told to "pause and purge the log."

Two minutes later, three black-badged agents from Division Epsilon entered the telemetry lab. No words. Just a data wipe, and a silence order.

"Do you want to keep your job, Dr. Park?" they asked. "Then you never received anything from Mars."

Park wasn't the only one.

At a listening post in Norway, a deep-space analyst named Hanna detected two separate beacons originating from Aletheia Base.

One went to Earth.

The other... was redirected.

To a private satellite array in low Mars orbit. An unregistered one.

The signature was familiar. It was a backdoor system—a relay used by a defunct Mars colonization group. A think tank that had quietly folded years ago. Or had it?

When Hanna filed a report, her access was revoked by morning. Her apartment had been searched. Her backups were deleted.

No one spoke of Mars anymore.

At 16:12 the next day, an internal memo was sent through the highest classified channels.

Subject: UNS-Charon Project Activation

Orders: Initiate deployment of Agent P.A.L.E.

Target Location: Aletheia Base

Objective: "Integration under pretext of Earth-based intervention. Monitor remaining subjects. Extract viable assets. Terminate contamination if necessary."

It wasn't signed.

It had no return path.

And no one who received it could confirm who issued the order.

Somewhere deep under Colorado, in a sealed black facility, a single screen glowed.

On it: Aletheia Base. Sol 21. Thirteen survivors.

Audio was live.

A voice spoke in the dark—cold, clinical, and male.

"They're beginning to see."

Behind the voice, monitors displayed brainwave patterns, emotional response charts, and something else—

—a seventeenth signature.

One that never came from Earth.

But had been there... since Sol 1.

"Prepare the vessel," the voice said.

"It's time to walk among them."

Sol 22

The morning was strangely calm.

No systems failed. No hallucinations. The air smelled less recycled, somehow. Elira half-expected another death—but nothing came.

Then the proximity alarm went off.

Ava raced to the north port window, rifle in hand. What she saw stopped her breath.

A figure.

Walking across the red plain.

No rover. No EVA suit.

Just... a man.

He walked without hesitation, boots crunching softly on Martian soil.

A sleek, black exosuit clung to his frame, segmented like bone armor but oddly flexible. A silver emblem glinted faintly on his chest: a spiral twisting inward, with a tiny human silhouette at the center.

He looked unbothered by the thin air, the cold, the radiation.

As if he belonged there.

He raised one hand. Not a wave—more like a signal. Or a greeting.

"I come from Earth."

They let him in.

Ava didn't lower the gun. Jonas refused to speak. Olivia kept one hand on the emergency lockdown switch the entire time.

The man removed his helmet. He was... ordinary. Pale skin. Cropped black hair. Icy gray eyes. No scars, no signs of exhaustion.

"My name is Lars. I was sent to respond to your emergency transmission."

Olivia's voice cracked slightly. "That message was only sent four days ago. There's no way—"

"Time is fluid where I come from," he said. "Earth heard. But not in time. So they sent me... another way."

He smiled.

It didn't reach his eyes.

He claimed to be part of a classified Earth response team, part of a dormant project known as Echo Umbra—an emergency measure never officially acknowledged.

> "Earth feared something like this might happen. That a mind exposed too long to Mars' silence could fracture. Lose sense of self. Develop... parallel thoughts."

He asked to see Kira's journal. Voss's last logs. The crime scenes.

He showed no reaction to the body reports. No disgust. Just fascination.

"You weren't just being observed," he said. "You were part of a stress experiment. One with a flaw."

Olivia's knuckles whitened. "Are you saying we were test subjects?"

He shook his head.

"I'm saying someone else hijacked your test. Someone not from Earth."

The others weren't convinced.

Jonas stared at Lar's suit for hours, muttering about seams that weren't real.

Ava ran a full biometric scan. No records. No match in any Earth registry.

Olivia asked for proof of Earth authority. He smiled again and said,

"Proof is a matter of belief."

But he knew things. Private logs. Kira's fears. Voss's childhood trauma. Things no one had ever recorded.

And then, worst of all, he asked:

"Which of you dreams in twos?"

That night, he spoke with Olivia alone.

The room was dark. His presence almost absorbed the light.

"One of your seven is not who they believe they are," he said. "They carry something foreign. Something old."

"Alien?" she asked.

He didn't answer. Just looked out the small round window, toward the dunes.

"There are two kinds of death, Commander. The kind you cause... and the kind you become."

He turned, and for a moment—just a flicker—his eyes reflected the light wrong.

Not like a human.

Like a predator's.

–That night, Jonas found the footage.

Security log from the airlock.

The system had never opened. No oxygen loss. No pressure change.

No entry at all.

And yet...Lar was inside.

Jonas didn't tell the others.

Not yet.

He just sat in the dark, watching the man who claimed to be from Earth sit calmly in the mess hall. Not eating. Not moving. Just waiting.

And smiling.

Sol 23

It began with the humming.

Soft at first—like the whine of ancient machinery hidden behind the walls.

Then it grew sharper. Too sharp. Like something alive was tuning into them.

Each surviving crew member reported strange symptoms:

Jonas heard whispers from the vents, calling him by the name of his dead brother.

Ava found her oxygen logs overwritten with ancient Greek text—which she could suddenly read.

Olivia dreamed of an impossible twin, watching her through the airlock glass.

And yet, none of it felt like madness.

It felt precise. Engineered.

Lar gathered them in the observation dome. His tone was soft. Almost parental.

"You've been contaminated. Not by a virus. Not by radiation.

But by proximity to something that predates us. Something that only reveals itself when belief collapses."

No one understood what he meant. But his words stayed lodged in their minds like seeds.

He gave them a box. No label. No markings.

"Put it in your sleeping quarters," he said. "Open it when you dream."

They found one in each room by nightfall.

Malik—once the crew's anchor—was already fraying.

He claimed his reflection was blinking out of sync with his own eyes.

He stopped sleeping. Spoke in murmurs. Sometimes in Latin, which he'd never studied.

One night Olivia found him sitting naked in the greenhouse, facing the hydroponic tanks.

"They're watching," he whispered. "From inside the lettuce."

When they asked him who "they" were, he answered:

"Us. Before we knew we were pretending to be human."

On Sol 24, Malik opened his box.

The rest of the crew found it the next morning—neatly placed on his desk. Inside: a black sphere, smooth as obsidian, still warm to the touch.

But Malik was gone.

His room was pristine. Nothing out of place—except a line carved into the metal wall with a scalpel:

"If your body can't hold the truth, it UNFOLDS you."

And the walls... were pulsing.

Like they were breathing.

Ava, searching for fresh water samples, found Malik's body among the plant roots.

But it wasn't just a body.

He'd been bent into a spiral. Not broken. Not mutilated. Reshaped—like his spine had uncoiled and rewrapped.

His face was pressed against the glass of the nutrient tank. His mouth agape, stuffed with seeds.

His eyes were gone, but somehow his expression still screamed.

On the glass, in breath-fog:

"I opened the box, and it opened me."

Lar.

He didn't panic. Didn't even flinch.

He looked at the twisted body as if it confirmed a theory.

"He was the first to see himself fully. A tragedy. But not unexpected."

Olivia nearly attacked him. "You knew this would happen!"

Lar only nodded once.

"The truth is not kind. It never has been."

"What truth?" Ava growled, shaking. "What the hell is happening to us?"

Lar gazed at the spiral Malik had become.

"You're not breaking down.

You're remembering what you were before Earth taught you to lie to yourselves."

That night, Jonas couldn't sleep. He played old comms logs—anything to ground himself.

But one file had changed.

A log from Sol 3, when Malik first arrived on Mars.

The voice was Malik's... at first.

Then halfway through, it distorted—into Lars Voice, perfectly.

"Arrival successful. They don't suspect it. Subject Malik will hold the signal."

"When the boxes open, we begin the return."

Jonas dropped the tablet.

His own box, still unopened, sat across the room.

Humming.

CHAPTER IV

The Archivist

Sol 25

For weeks, he'd been in the background.

His name is rarely spoken aloud. His job is too technical, too unglamorous.

But now—he mattered.

Elias Verin

Communications and Signal Integrity Officer.

Tasked with maintaining the audio-visual logs, comms, and system time-syncs.

The person who should have known when the message to Earth was sent—and if anyone ever received it.

Malik's twisted corpse was sealed in chamber C. No one would go near it.

But Lar ... he remained helpful. Gentle. Quiet.

He took on cooking duty. Cleaned the hydroponics. Sat with Ava during her panic spells.

The more horrific things became, the more human Lar seemed.

But Elias...

Elias started changing.

They noticed strange things about Elias:

He began muttering radio codes under his breath—discontinued ones, from dead satellites.

He stopped eating in the mess hall, instead reviewing days-old footage at 4x speed, eyes wide, veins in his temple throbbing.

He claimed the footage was changing itself.

"Someone's editing it backwards," he told Olivia. "The deaths are playing before they happen."

"That's impossible," Ava snapped.

"No. That's the point," he whispered. "That's what they want—for us to question the order of time."

Jonas found Elias asleep at the comms panel.

The screen showed live footage... of Elias himself... sleeping at the panel.

But in the background—deep in the hallway—Malik stood. Head bent. Staring directly at the lens.

Jonas screamed.

Elias didn't wake.

When the others arrived, the feed had gone blank.

Elias denied everything. Claimed someone was playing with archived data.

When asked who, he answered:

"Whoever we buried in the soil here.

It's not a person. It's a recording."

Ava and Olivia found a hidden folder on the main server, titled: REHEARSAL_01.

Inside: dozens of videos.

All of them were re-creations of the crew's deaths.

Some hadn't happened yet.

Some were from angles that shouldn't exist—corner ceiling views, inside private quarters, even inside their helmets.

The timestamps were corrupted.

All signed by one user: VERIN.EX.

When confronted, Elias laughed.

"You think I made them? I'm the one trying to keep them from overwriting us!"

"Them?" Olivia asked.

Elias stared at her.

"Don't you feel it? Like you're being recorded backward? Like someone's watching you from a time that hasn't happened yet?"

Then he smiled.

"That's the real message we sent. We didn't reach Earth. We reached something else."

Sol 26

Jonas stopped sleeping.

Not out of fear—but out of surveillance. He took shifts in the comms room to keep an eye on Elias, scribbling notes in his journal in tight, manic handwriting.

"He talks to the static."

"He records nothing and says it's everything."

"He's writing something in binary on the walls."

Elias barely acknowledged him. He spent all his time reconfiguring the radio bands—detuning them into frequencies that sounded like breathing. He claimed it wasn't white noise.

It was a conversation.

"They're in the static," he told Jonas. "You just don't have the ears for it."

Ava tried to review Malik's final hours.

Gone.

All of it.

The footage from every camera in Malik's vicinity for the final 12 hours had been corrupted, overwritten with a black screen and low hissing noise—like muffled growling underwater.

Only one person had access clearance to those logs:

Elias Verin.

When confronted, Elias smirked.

"You're assuming the footage ever existed at all.

What if memory is just... shared hallucination?"

Later, Jonas discovered blood dripping from the ventilation shaft near Elias's quarters.

They unscrewed the grating—expecting another body.

Instead: a tangle of wires, weaved together into a lattice shaped like a spinal cord. At the base, a small carved metal tag:

T-081: "REHEARSAL COMPLETE"

Jonas held it in a shaking hand.

"What the hell is this?"

Elias, standing behind him, simply said:

"A rehearsal space. That's all this place is."

One night, Olivia found Elias sitting alone in the oxygen garden, facing the reflective interior of the water tank.

He didn't look up.

"Do you ever wonder if you died on the way here?" he asked. "And this is just the story your brain plays before you rot?"

She didn't respond.

"Because that's what they're watching," he said. "They're not watching us. They're watching the version of us that thinks it's still alive."

Then he pressed his hand against the glass—and the reflection didn't match his movement.

It hesitated. Smiled. Then mirrored him again.

Olivia stepped back.

Ava compiled a list:

Elias had been near every location before the deaths occurred.

He was caught muttering timestamps before anyone died—timestamps that later matched.

He'd created fake footage of Jonas's death—even though Jonas was still alive.

The surveillance logs were disappearing faster than anyone could verify them.

Still—no one could catch him doing anything wrong.

lar, meanwhile, remained the calm center of gravity. The one voice of reason. He reassured Ava:

"Elias is broken. Not dangerous. There's a difference."

But Jonas wasn't convinced.

"What if he's not broken?" Jonas whispered to olivia. "What if he's the only one not infected?"

Then: the radio tower malfunctioned. Fried from the inside.

Traced to a looped surge from the relay terminal.

One person had clearance.

Elias.

"You think I'd sabotage the only way out?" Elias growled. "I didn't touch it. It died on its own. Just like the message we sent."

When asked what he meant, he grinned.

"The message wasn't corrupted on the way out.

It was answered."

Jonas stole Elias's private journal.

Inside: pages and pages of mirrored handwriting, timestamps, sketches of the team—but with their skulls removed and machinery inside.

One page showed Malik's twisted corpse drawn days before the death occurred. Labeled:

"M-02 Spiral Expression // Externalized Doubt"

Another showed Jonas—eyes gouged, suspended in zero-G above his bunk.

"J-03: Collapse of Observation."

Jonas dropped the notebook.

The date next to his drawing was tomorrow.

Ava tried to delete the journal. The files are duplicated.

Jonas tried to warn olivia—she told him to sleep.

That night, Jonas watched the footage from Sol 10. The day before the first murder.

In the corner of the frame—Elias is standing behind Malik, staring.

Still. Silent.

But his shadow... doesn't move with his body.

It crawls up the wall. Across the ceiling. Into the vents.

And vanishes.

Jonas hit pause.

The timestamp blinked:

00:00:00

Sol 27

Olivia sat in the medical bay, staring at a photograph.

She didn't remember taking it.

It showed the full crew standing on the Martian surface—sixteen of them, suited and smiling.

But two things were wrong.

1. She was missing from the photo.

2. There were seventeen people in it.

Ava woke up screaming.

She'd had a dream—a simple one. Dinner with Olivia and Jonas. Laughter. Old Earth music in the background.

But when she told Olivia about it that morning, Olivia looked pale.

"That never happened," she whispered. "You haven't eaten with me in three days."

"Yes, I have," Ava snapped. "We shared that synthetic lasagna crap. You made fun of Jonas's snoring."

"Ava... I haven't slept in my room for three days. There's blood in the wall from Malik's scream. I've been staying in hydroponics."

They both fell silent.
Each was completely certain.
And completely wrong.

In the control deck, Jonas played back footage from Sol 21.

It showed Ava and Olivia in the kitchen—arguing about Elias, about whether to sedate him.

But Olivia's voice in the video was slightly off.
Her cadence too even.
Her movements looped every 14 seconds.
And then... it switched.

In mid-sentence, she vanished from the frame—replaced by lar , who said the same words she had, verbatim.

Jonas froze the footage.

"They're being overwritten," he muttered. "They're... merging."

Later that day, Ava found Olivia in the oxygen chamber.

She was humming a lullaby Ava remembered from childhood.

"My mom sang that to me," Ava whispered.

"I know," Olivia replied. "You told me. When we were kids."

Ava blinked.

"We met during the mission training—two years ago."

Olivia smiled. Soft. Almost apologetic.

"You've forgotten again."

Ava backed away.

But when she checked the oxygen logs... they said Olivia hadn't entered the chamber all day.

Yet the humidity monitor showed two breathing bodies inside at 14:12 p.m.

Ava began compiling a memory journal—trying to fact-check her own mind.

But on every page, her handwriting changed styles.

Some entries were dated with a Martian calendar the team had never used.

One entry said:

"Olivia is Lar. Or Lar is Olivia's dream."

Another said:

"We buried Olivia. Sol 19."

She confronted Olivia, trembling.

"Were you... ever dead?"

Olivia looked her dead in the eye and said:

"Twice."

In the storage deck, Olivia found something chilling.

A cryo-box labeled "Subject: O-LV02".

Inside: a Martian suit. Her size. Her tag. Her biometrics.

Untouched.

But she remembered wearing it.

On the first walk.

The serial tag didn't match any known suit record.

She turned to Jonas.

"Why do I feel like I'm the backup?" she whispered.

Jonas didn't respond.

He was watching another file—one that showed Olivia entering the base 13 minutes after she supposedly walked out of it.

Two Olivias.
One gone by the next frame.
That night, Olivia looked at herself in the mirror.
For a moment, her reflection didn't move.
It watched her.
Then it smiled, gently... and whispered in her own voice:
"They'll delete you next. Make sure you're the version that survives."

She blinked.
The reflection returned to normal.
But there were fingerprints on the glass.
From the inside.

CHAPTER V

We were Not The First

Sol 28

Jonas sat alone in the comms room, combing through archived telemetry. He hadn't slept. Not because of fear—but because of patterns.

There was something wrong with the data from Sol 1.

Too clean. Too consistent.

The entry logs for atmospheric pressure, radio fluctuations, solar interference—they all matched the baseline simulation data used in training.

Word for word.

Number for number.

Exactly.

He pulled a hidden server partition—a locked directory marked LOG_GHOST_XX1.

Inside: compressed data logs.

Dated six years before their arrival.

No mention of them in NASA's briefings. No press release. No memorial.

The mission header read:

ARES-I INITIATIVE: CREW 01 – MARS ENTRY POINT ALPHA

Status: REDACTED

Final Entry Timestamp: "Mission Compromised: 73 hrs, 22 mins after landing."

He opened the final log.

Audio only.

"...we are not alone. Requesting emergency extraction. It's looping. They're... making us again. Please. There's another version of me in the hall and he's smiling—he shouldn't know how to smile like that—"

[UNINTELLIGIBLE SCREAMING]

"Shut it down. Delete this recording. Bury us with it."

Meanwhile, Olivia paced outside the storage chamber, heart hammering.

She approached Lar—her most trusted anchor in the unraveling chaos.

> "Why weren't we told about Ares-I?" she asked.

Lar blinked. Genuine confusion.

"There was no Ares-I," he said. "This is the first mission."

"Then explain the logs Jonas found. Explain why there's another mission's telemetry under our own timestamp headers."

Lar's eyes darkened.

"Maybe you're misremembering."

"I'm not."

"Or maybe," Lar said quietly, "you're remembering too much."

Ava and Olivia followed Jonas to the lower deck—beneath the cryo storage unit Lar had strictly forbidden them to access.

Behind the wall was a sealed hatch.

Jonas pried it open.

Inside: a sealed crew capsule. The exterior faded, scrawled with words in blood or something darker:

WE NEVER LEFT.

YOU ARE OUR REWRITE.

Inside the capsule were six seats—five still filled with skeletons in decomposed suits.
Each wore the same mission patch:
ARES-I | INITIATION PROTOCOL

And behind them, engraved on a scorched metal panel:
"Observe. Erase. Repeat."
Then Jonas found the final horror:
A mirrored photo panel—crew headshots from Ares-I.
He dropped it.
Olivia picked it up.
There she was.
Face identical to hers. Same eyes. Same smile. Labeled:
DR. OLIVIA MARIN - COMMUNICATIONS OFFICER

Ava too.
Lar.
Elias.
All of them.
Exactly the same. Not ancestors. Not relatives.
Copies.
Or iterations.

Lar stepped into the room behind them.He looked at the skeletons.
Calm.
Thoughtful.
"You weren't supposed to find this."

Olivia stood, shaking.

"What are we, Lar?"

Lar didn't blink.

"This version... is still stabilizing. Don't ruin it."

He walked away without another word.

Later that night, Jonas noticed something in the lower terminal:

A countdown embedded in the background system loop.It ticked down as he watched.

Underneath it:

"Version: 07"

And below that:

"Corruption Threshold: 39% — Recommendation: Terminate."

Sol 29

The surviving crew had begun avoiding eye contact. Conversations were clipped, suspicious. The tension between Olivia, Ava, Jonas, Lar, and the others—Sierra, Griggs, Kelman,etc.—felt like a stretched wire under frostbite. No one could remember the last time they laughed. Sleep was stolen, shallow. And everywhere lingered the question none dared ask aloud:

Who would be next?

No one trusted Elias anymore. His silence had grown stranger. He spoke to himself under his breath, and when he did speak aloud, it was in fragments—quoting mission logs that had never been written. Jonas insisted they keep him locked in the med-bay. Lar disagreed.

That night, one of them vanished.

Griggs was last seen heading toward the auxiliary greenhouse to check the filtration lines.

Sierra had nodded to him in the corridor. He smiled back—tight-lipped, too calm.

He never returned.

At 03:41 Martian Sol Time, Ava and Olivia found a trail—not blood, but shards of fingernails, spaced evenly along the hallway. They followed it in dead silence, flashlights swinging over the red-dusted metal floor.

At the greenhouse entryway, the lights flickered. One of the panels was broken open, the wires sparking. The inside reeked of rust and something sourer—flesh, but days old.

Jonas pushed the door fully open.

And vomited.

Griggs' Body.

He was strung up from the greenhouse support beams with oxygen tubing—his own, likely torn from his backup tank. His skin had been peeled in symmetrical lines, the fat sculpted away from the muscle. On his face: a look of frozen horror, his lips split wide and his eyes open so far it looked like the lids had been cut.

There was no sign of a struggle.

A note had been pinned into the tissue above his navel using a surgical blade. Jonas had to tug it free. It was written in jagged strokes with something that might've been blood—or something darker.

"HE TALKED IN HIS SLEEP."

"HE WASN'T SUPPOSED TO REMEMBER."

Back in the core habitat, panic erupted like wildfire in a sealed room.

Kelman accused Elias—pointing to his bizarre behavior, the muttering, the isolated murmuring in the dark.

"He's quoting dead logs," Kelman hissed. "He's not even trying to hide it anymore."

Lar snapped back: "We have no proof. Everyone here is breaking. You think that's abnormal? Look at you—you've been collecting bone samples like souvenirs."

Elias sat calmly, his fingers interlocked. He smiled at Olivia. A small, innocent smile.

"I didn't kill Griggs," he whispered. "But I heard him die. I was dreaming. The sound was...wet. Like someone stirring meat with a stick."

Later that night, Olivia stood at the mirror in the hygiene bay. She stared at herself, trying to focus.

Had her face always looked like this?

Had her voice always carried this rasp at the end of every breath?

Behind her, a whisper.

"Did you sleepwalk last night?"

She spun.

No one was there.

She locked the mirror cabinet out of instinct, then opened it again a moment later—and saw a fingerprint on the inside of the glass.

It was not hers.

Sierra began screaming at nothing the next morning. She stood in the common room with her tablet, pointing at the walls.

"It wasn't me! I didn't write this! I didn't write this in my sleep!"

Everyone gathered around.

Her tablet now contained pages and pages of text—typed while she slept. An account of Griggs' death, described in horrifying detail. Even the internal injuries

Kelman had found.

She had no memory of it.

Her hands trembled. "I—I haven't even been to the greenhouse since Sol 26."

Lar took the tablet from her, gently. "Then someone used your login."

Sierra whispered, "But who knew my password?"

Jonas reviewed the hallway footage later that day.

The camera watching the greenhouse corridor—the one Griggs had taken—glitched at exactly 03:16.

When the feed returned, there was a figure in the background. Standing near the water tank. Not moving.

Only visible for one frame.

And in that frame, Jonas paused the footage and slowly enhanced it.

It looked like Elias.

But the eyes were too wide. The mouth is too far apart. As if whoever—or whatever—wore Elias's skin hadn't practiced the smile enough.

Ava, still shaken from the discovery, tried to distract herself by scrolling through old surface mission images on a shared database.

She paused on one taken on Sol 9—of the whole team, suited up on the red sands.

There was something off.

In the background, nearly a kilometer away, standing at the horizon line, was a dark figure.

Suitless.

Unmoving.

Facing the camera.

Sol 30

The station had gone silent.

Tense, restrained, like the entire structure was holding its breath. No one moved without announcing it. No one went to the restroom alone. They locked their doors, slept with multitools under their pillows, and whispered like the walls were listening.

Jonas volunteered to take the 0200 perimeter check.

He needed the silence, he told himself.

What he didn't tell anyone was that he'd begun suspecting Sierra.

Ever since she screamed about the typed confession, she hadn't looked the same. She muttered under her breath, wrote things in symbols on her arms, stared too long at empty rooms.

So when she slipped out of the sleeping bay at 01:48, Jonas followed her.

What he found would scar him for life.

The outer corridor lights flickered again. Always in that spot.

Jonas crouched near the edge of the corridor and leaned against the cool metal. He could hear Sierra breathing — slow, rhythmic, but shallow. He could see her silhouette in the glass.

But she wasn't alone.

Someone was in there with her.

At first, Jonas thought it was Lar — the posture was similar. But something about the movement was wrong. Too smooth. Almost like it was being puppeteered from the inside.

Then the silhouette raised an object — thin, sharp.

Sierra turned.

She whispered something.

The figure responded by plunging the instrument into her shoulder.

Jonas stumbled forward and slammed against the glass.

The killer didn't flinch.

Inside, Sierra screamed, scrambling back across the greenhouse floor, blood smearing into the soil trench beside her. She tried to crawl toward the door.

The killer followed, calm, collected — with surgical grace.

He dragged her by the ankle.

He turned her over.

Jonas could see her face now — eyes wide, mouth foaming, trying to scream, to signal, anything.

The killer held up a scalpel and inserted it beneath the skin of her cheek, slicing horizontally with slow, perfect precision. The skin peeled away like an orange rind.

He was smiling.

Jonas shouted for help.

He pounded the comm button.

Nothing. Dead frequency. Again.

He screamed at the glass.

Inside, Sierra's screams died in her throat. The killer reached inside her mouth and broke her jaw sideways with one hand — a wet, cracking sound that made Jonas retch against the wall.

Blood pooled into the soil.

The killer lifted her hand, took the scalpel again, and began removing her fingernails, one by one, lining them up beside her body.

He carved symbols into her skin — downward spiral patterns, precise slashes. A kind of message.

Jonas realized he wasn't trying to hide.

He was staging her.

When the killer stood and turned, Jonas caught his first full look:

It was Elias.

But something was... off.

His face was stretched into a grin too wide. His uniform was covered in soil and gore, but his hands were clean. His eyes locked onto Jonas through the glass — cold, dead, knowing.

And he nodded.

Just once.

Then calmly walked to the far exit and disappeared into the red dawn light bleeding through the glass.

Jonas collapsed.

...

It took twenty minutes to gather the others.

By then, Sierra's body had gone stiff, twisted in her final death pose — arms bent backwards, legs folded beneath her like a doll. The symbols in her skin shimmered where the blood was still drying.

Kelman confirmed her tongue had been removed. Carefully. Precisely.

Ava kept whispering: "Why did he smile at you? Why would he let you see it?"

Jonas had no answer.

Only one thing made sense:

"He wanted me to watch."

CHAPTER VI

The Walls Know

The greenhouse was sealed off.

The stench of death still clung to the air despite the filtration systems running at full force. No one wanted to speak of what they saw, but it hovered unspoken between them like smoke in a pressurized room — thick, choking, impossible to ignore.

Jonas sat alone in the storage bay, wrists bound with utility cord. His hands still trembled from what he'd witnessed — or claimed to witness. He couldn't stop repeating it in his head: Elias. The scalpel. The smile. The way he'd nodded before walking away, like a showman concluding an act.

But now Elias was gone.

Vanished without a trace.

And Jonas was the only one left with blood on his clothes.

"He followed her," Jonas kept whispering. "He went in before me. I swear to God, he smiled at me. He wanted me to see."

But no one believed him.

Lar stood in the command deck, arms crossed tightly over his chest. He had taken charge after Sierra's death — quietly, but unmistakably. The others looked at him now. He was calm, direct, and seemed to be the only one thinking clearly.

Olivia leaned against the console, her face pale and tight. "So Jonas followed her, saw the murder, and... conveniently forgot to call anyone until after she was dead?"

"It doesn't make sense," Ava muttered. "Why would Elias just disappear?"

Lar exhaled through his nose and said softly, "Because he knew Jonas would take the fall."

They all turned to look at him.

"If Jonas is telling the truth," he said, "then Elias wanted us to turn on him. That's the kind of game this is now."

Kelman poured through the logs, the camera feeds, the movement trackers.

Nothing.

The cameras in the greenhouse corridor blinked out during the murder, as they had the last time. The footage restarted at 03:52 — thirty seconds after Elias supposedly left.

There was no exit footage.

No trace of him leaving the module.

It was as if Elias had simply melted into the floor.

Meanwhile, Jonas' screams on the comm system didn't register at all. No audio logs. No outgoing signal. The software had been wiped clean.

"Who has that kind of access?" Olivia whispered.

No one answered.

Lar visited Jonas privately. He didn't bring weapons. He didn't accuse.

He just sat across from him, arms resting on his knees.

"You have to help me," he said. "If there's something you're not telling us, now's the time. Because if I can't convince them you're not the killer... they will leave you to rot."

Jonas looked up, eyes hollow. "He was enjoying it, Lar. He was careful. Precise. Like he'd done it before. And the way he looked at me... I've never felt so small. So helpless."

Lar gave a slow nod.

"Then help me find him before someone else dies."

That night, the power blinked.

Not in the whole station — just one module.

The Hydration Lab, where Kelman was running tests on the irrigation tanks.

He had refused to pair up, insisting he needed time alone. The others allowed it reluctantly. Lar was about to check on him when the lights dimmed and a scream echoed through the floor vents.

By the time they pried open the door, it was already too late.

Kelman was boiled from the inside out — his body crumpled beside a rupture in the pressurized water line. His mouth was open in a silent scream, and his eyes had exploded from the heat.

Someone had overridden the temp regulator and locked the door from the outside.

And on the glass, written in vapor:

"HE STILL DOESN'T KNOW HE DID IT."

It seemed like the whatever was behind the murders wasn't hiding, it was communicating, it was leaving a message through his inhumane acts

---

The group splintered further.

Ava accused Jonas of hacking the systems — "He worked in diagnostics. He could wipe logs."

Olivia broke down and wept in the med-bay, repeating "Elias isn't gone. He's here. He's still here."

Jonas, still restrained, banged his head against the wall until Lar pulled him away.

But Lar was changing, too. His calmness now bordered on obsession. He didn't sleep. He started cross-referencing every crewmember's logs, mapping their movements, memorizing voice patterns from the comm records. The only one still trying to hold the threads together.

"We're not fighting a killer," he muttered one night. "We're fighting someone who doesn't believe they're killing."

That night, Olivia woke in her bunk to find her tablet open on her chest. The screen was on. A message blinked.

From an unknown account:

"It's you next."

She dropped it with a yelp and ran to Ava, who clutched her and whispered, "We have to leave him. We have to lock Jonas out. We'll die if we don't."

Olivia shook her head. "I'm not sure it's him. What if we're wrong?"

They heard a knock on the outside of the sleeping module door.

Just one knock.

Then silence.

Sol 32

They heard it first during a systems check. A whisper.

Static-wrapped. Half-swallowed by the transmission, like it was leaking through the gaps in the signal architecture. Ava froze in the middle of her diagnostic sweep, one gloved finger hovering over the interface panel. She stared at the headset as the hiss returned, then —

unmistakably:

"Jonas."

Just the name. Soft, rasped. Not a command. Not a warning.

A summons.

Ava didn't tell the others at first. Who would believe her?

But that night, Olivia sat upright in her bunk, trembling and drenched in sweat. She had woken to someone breathing into her ear.

No one was there.

Her comm unit blinked red — active.

She played back the feed. Ten seconds of dead air.

Then:

"Olivia... do you remember the room with the missing door?"

The voice was Elias's. But... it wasn't. Too hollow. Slowed slightly, as if dragged through a corrupted algorithm.

She didn't sleep the rest of the night.

Lar moved like a man unraveling in slow motion. His precision remained, his voice still calm. But there was a wildness in his eyes now — he was staring into shadows longer than necessary, blinking at nothing, snapping his fingers in random rhythms, like keeping a beat only he could hear.

He gathered everyone at the common area — what was left of them.

"We're being watched," he said. "Not through cameras. Through us. It's using the comms. Not to speak. To listen. To learn."

Jonas, still bound, chuckled darkly. "You sound just like me now."

Lar didn't look at him.

"I think Elias is still here," Lar said. "But not physically. Not anymore. He's in the station."

No one laughed.

Later that night, the screams started.

Not over comms.

From beneath the station.

It sounded like someone was trapped in the maintenance floor — the crawlspace used for routing wiring and coolant pipes. They heard slamming fists, muffled sobbing, the clang of someone scraping metal with their nails.

Lar went down with a flashlight and came back up ten minutes later, pale and shaking.

"There's no one there," he whispered.

Then he vomited on the floor.

The Second Signal

At 03:42, the station received a transmission ping.

Not from Earth.

From inside the habitat's internal comm system.

It routed through every speaker, every headset, every device. A feedback loop of static, screams, and beneath it — again — the voice.

But this time, it was chanting.

"You're all already dead. You're all already dead. You're all already—"

It looped seven times before Lar ripped out the core processor and manually shut it down.

They sat in silence.

Jonas began sobbing in the corner.

Ava stared at the ceiling.

Olivia whispered: "That wasn't Elias. That wasn't even a person."

At dawn, the air recycling unit began to scream.

Not beep. Scream.

A horrible metallic shriek as the ventilation fans struggled against something caught deep in the return shaft. Olivia was the first to reach it — Lar close behind, prying the outer panel off with a crowbar.

What tumbled out was not a corpse.

It was Ava.

Broken, barely breathing, folded wrong — like someone had tried to fit her into a space too small, too fast, with no regard for anatomy. One of her arms was dislocated and twisted behind her back. Her left eye was missing. Her lips were torn from the corners, pulled into a grotesque, ragged smile.

But she was alive.

She gasped when the cold air hit her skin, jerking like a marionette. Olivia screamed. Lar dropped to his knees and tried to hold her still.

"Ava. Ava—who did this? Who did this?!"

She blinked up at them. One working eye, wide, glassy. Her lips moved. Blood bubbled through her teeth.

Then she whispered:

"E–Elias. He's."

Lar froze.

"What?"

Her breathing rattled. "He's still... inside... but there's more now. Something else... something ancient... it hollowed him out."

"Where is he?"

Her mouth trembled. "Behind the mirror. It's watching us through the reflection. We're the rehearsal."

She began to laugh.

Horrible, gurgling, wet laughter. Olivia had to hold her mouth shut to stop it.

And on her stomach, carved into the skin with surgical precision — not a message, but a face.

Elias's face.

Smiling.

The phrase clung to Lar like frostbite:
"Behind the mirror."

Not in it. Not near it.

Behind it.

He stood now in the med-bay, the one place on the station that still felt sterile — or at least had tried to. Blood had dried in the corners. Ava's mangled laughter still echoed in the corridors. The mirror above the sink, spiderwebbed with hairline cracks, reflected his face with eerie sharpness.

Olivia entered, eyes red from lack of sleep. She said nothing, just stood beside him. They both looked into the mirror.

Lar reached up and touched it.

It was cold.

And then — he felt it.

A vibration. Subtle. Alive.

"It's humming," he muttered.

Olivia whispered, "It's listening."

Later that night, Lar returned alone.

He unscrewed the mirror from the wall. It came off easily. Too easily.

Behind it: a hollow space, about three feet deep.

And in the dark, something moved.

Lar flinched back, almost falling — but nothing came out. When he steadied his light and peered inside, he saw something even worse than an intruder.

Another mirror.

Not glass — but a panel. Seamless. Reflective. Polished like obsidian.

And in that reflection... Lar wasn't alone.

A second figure stood behind him.

He turned — no one.

Looked back — still there.

Closer now.

It wore his face.

While Lar dissected the wall, Olivia began noticing inconsistencies.

Her own reflection didn't match her movements.

She would tilt her head left — the reflection twitched, like it needed a second to catch up. When she blinked, it sometimes didn't.

She stopped using mirrors. Avoided her reflection. But then the glass of her tablet began to fog when she walked by, even when it was off.

And worse, she began hearing her own voice whispering in the night.

"You're not Olivia."

"You've never been Olivia."

With tools, Lar widened the wall cavity behind the mirror until he could squeeze inside.

What he found made him gasp.

A corridor.

A hidden one — thin, curving slightly, the walls covered in a black reflective surface, like a ribcage of mirrors.

And they were all active.

They showed scenes. Not reflections — recordings.

Ava screams.

Sierra dying.

Kelman being shoved into the water tank.

The footage twisted, looped, repeated in unnatural rhythms. Sometimes they stuttered — and the figures in the mirrors looked directly at Lar.

"We're not watching memories," he whispered. "They're watching us."

Behind him, Olivia's voice cracked: "Why does mine show things I don't remember doing?"

In one panel, Lar finally saw Elias.

Or what was left of him.

The figure looked like Elias, moved like Elias — but the skin was stretched, twitching. The mouth was too wide. The eyes blacker than the void outside. It was speaking to something off-camera.

But no audio came through.

Lar leaned closer, trying to read his lips.

Then the figure turned, slowly, deliberately.

And pointed directly at Lar.

Not at the reflection — at him.

The screen spider-cracked.

And something knocked from the other side.

Lar and Olivia tried to leave the corridor — but the hatch had sealed behind them. The lighting flickered, and now the walls no longer showed past recordings.

Now they showed versions of themselves.

Not real versions.

Twisted ones. Lar smiling with blood-soaked hands. Olivia dissecting Jonas like a doll. Other selves. Possible selves.

Olivia began to cry.

"I can't tell which one is me anymore."

Lar whispered:

"Maybe that's the point."

At last, they found the final panel.

No reflection.

No movement.

Just words etched in what looked like blood, across the black surface:

"YOU BROUGHT US HERE. YOU DON'T REMEMBER."

"YOUR FACES ARE OUR MASKS."

"WHEN YOU SLEEP, WE PRACTICE."

Sol 34

Jonas had been confined to the storage module — a narrow, insulated room with no windows, one vent, and a single flickering light that didn't blink in any regular rhythm.

He'd stopped speaking aloud hours ago.

Not because he didn't have anything to say.

But because someone else was already talking.

To him.

From within him.

At first, it had sounded like his own thoughts. Just... a bit off. Like hearing your voice through an old tape.

"You didn't kill them."

"They made you forget."

"She had to die."

He tried to ignore it. Focused on breathing. Counting. Remembering Earth — the taste of air in spring, the sound of his sister's laugh.

But the voice grew louder. Familiar. Comforting. It called itself Elias now.

"We understand each other, Jonas."

"They broke you. I'm here to fix it."

Sometimes it used his mother's voice.

Other times... no voice at all. Just pressure. Like thoughts pushed into him from behind his own skull.

He screamed once. But the walls swallowed it.

He wasn't sure how long he'd been in the room.

There was no clock. No schedule.

Only the light — blinking like Morse code. Random. Taunting.

He began marking time by the rhythm of the voice.
At first, hours of silence.
Then whispers.
Then arguments.
Two voices. Not just one anymore.
One voice pleading.
The other commanding.
"He belongs to us."

"He wasn't supposed to see. He wasn't supposed to wake up."

Jonas pressed his hands to his ears until blood trickled down his neck.
They laughed.
He began seeing memories that weren't his.
Standing over Ava's bed. Watching Olivia sleep. Lifting the wrench.
But the hands weren't his.
They looked like his. But they moved wrong — like puppets.
And sometimes, when he blinked, he saw his reflection smiling when he wasn't.
He scratched at the wall. Over and over.
Eventually, he carved a message in his own blood, dragging broken fingernails across the aluminum.
"I AM NOT JONAS."
From the other side of the station, Olivia watched the live feed from the storage module.
Jonas sat cross-legged on the floor, humming something tuneless. His eyes were shut. Occasionally, he'd flinch like something brushed his shoulder.

Then he opened his mouth and, for one terrifying moment, spoke in Elias's exact voice:

"It's almost ready."

"They'll all wear us."

Olivia shut off the screen.

"Lar," she whispered. "He's splitting. We have to do something."

Lar didn't answer.

He was staring at his reflection in a puddle of blood, watching it blink out of sync.

Jonas had one moment of clarity.

A single second where the voices stopped, and everything went still.

He looked into the corner of the room — where the shadow always lingered — and whispered:

"What are you?"

The shadow stepped forward.

It didn't speak.

It didn't need to.

Jonas began to scream.

The kind of scream that never ends.

Sol 36

Lar stood outside the storage module with a prybar in hand.

The hatch was jammed.

Or sealed, he thought grimly. From the inside. No response from Jonas in hours. Not since the scream.

Olivia begged him not to go in alone.

"If something's in there with him—"

"Then it's too late for him either way," Lar had replied. "I need to see it for myself."

She gave him one last look, hollow-eyed. Then stepped back.

With a groan of warped metal, the door cracked open.

Darkness hit him like a wall.

The light overhead was shattered, hanging in pieces like a broken jaw. Glass crunched under his boots.

And the smell—putrid, metallic, human and not, like rusted meat sealed too long in something meant to stay sterile.

"Jonas...?"

No answer.

Just the tick-tick-tick of the broken fan in the vent above.

And the walls.

Lar turned on his headlamp.

That's when he saw it.

The walls. All four.

Covered in writing.

Hundreds of overlapping phrases — scratched, gouged, and smeared across every inch of space.

Not just in blood. Not only.

Some written with teeth marks.

Some finger-painted in a mixture of bile and something dark and tar-like.

He moved closer.

"WE WERE NEVER ALONE."

"THE AIR BREATHES BACK."

"I AM NOT JONAS."
"HE IS WATCHING THROUGH THE BONE."

Lar's hand trembled as he raised his light.

Dozens of eyes were drawn across the ceiling — in red, black, brown. Childlike. Huge.

Each one staring straight down.

At the center of the room, Jonas's blanket lay in a crumpled pile.

No body.

Just a single handprint.

On the ceiling.

Upside down.

Then something whispered. Not from the room. From the writing itself.

The words rippled — literally. Lar leaned in, heart hammering.

"Laaaar..."

Not Jonas's voice. Not Elias's.

His own voice.

Mocking.

He backed away, stumbling.

The fan above him clicked — then shrieked.

And something wet dropped onto his shoulder.

He looked up.

Saw nothing.

Felt everything.

On the way out, Lar fell against the far wall — his head connecting with a panel hard enough to split his scalp.

Dazed, blinking blood, he saw the message directly above where Jonas had slept.

One he hadn't noticed before. Deep. Carved through paint and metal.

"THEY'RE USING OUR FACES."

"WHEN WE DREAM, THEY LEARN."

"I'M NOT WRITING THIS."

"HELP."

Then, below it, written in fresh blood — still wet:
"LAR. OPEN YOUR EYES."

His breath caught.

He turned back to the door—ready to run—when he saw his own name.

Dozens of times. Hidden under other phrases. As if they'd been etched over. Rewritten.

A message forming in reverse, as though someone had been slowly building it all along:
"LAR. YOU. WERE. FIRST."

Sol 37

He didn't speak about the room.

Not the blood. Not the writing. Not the handprint on the ceiling.

He told Olivia the hatch was jammed, and Jonas was gone. "No trace," he said. "He probably broke through a vent."

She watched him for a long time. Too long.

"Did you... find anything else?"

Lar blinked. Shook his head. "No. Just dark. Smelled like rot. Nothing useful."

A pause.

Olivia turned away first.

He exhaled only when she was out of the corridor. That's when his knees almost gave out.

He hadn't lied.

He'd just left things out.

All the important things.

That night, Lar lay on his bunk, staring at the ceiling.

He saw the words again. The phrases. Scratched into the walls by Jonas's bleeding fingers.

Some of them had changed since he saw them.

He was sure of it.

He'd memorized one line—"WHEN WE DREAM, THEY LEARN."

Now it echoed in his head as:

"WHEN YOU SLEEP, WE EAT."

He sat up, sweating.

And that's when he saw it:

A smear of blood on the inside of his sleeve.

He hadn't noticed it earlier.

He hadn't touched anything... had he?

The next day, Olivia approached him again.

Her expression had hardened.

"I checked the logs. Jonas didn't have access to the internal panels. He couldn't have disappeared into a vent without setting off a breach alarm."

Lar swallowed.

"Then he set one off and bypassed it. Or Elias helped."

Olivia didn't look convinced.

"And that message you showed me—the one you said Jonas carved—why didn't you bring back a scan?"

"Didn't think to."

"You always think to."

Lar met her gaze. Calm. Cool. Steady.
Too steady.
He began seeing himself in the reflections again.
But only when he blinked.
Split-second moments where his reflection didn't mirror him. It lagged, just a little. Smiled when he didn't.
One night, walking past the decontamination bay, he caught a glimpse in the chrome plating.
His reflection had blood running from its eyes.
It grinned.
And whispered:
"You went into the room, Lar. But you didn't come back alone."
A message appeared on his private tablet. No sender.
Just one line:
"You carved it."
He tried deleting it.
It reappeared.
He smashed the tablet.
The next morning, a new one was already in his locker — preloaded. Waiting.
Same message on the lock screen.
"You carved it."
Sleep is the Enemy
He stopped sleeping.
Every time he drifted, he dreamt of words.

Not voices. Words. Endless walls of them. Scrawled across skin, across space, across stars.

And always, one word was in the center.

LAR

Sometimes he saw it stitched into a cadaver.

Sometimes carved into his own teeth.

"Lar," she said quietly one night, after everyone had gone to sleep. "You're changing."

He didn't answer.

"You didn't come back alone, did you?"

Still, he said nothing.

And Olivia whispered:

> "If I look into your eyes right now... whose are they?"

CHAPTER VII

The Silent Room

Sol 38

They found Rhea in the Hydroponics Chamber — where the only sound was the gentle bubbling of nutrient tanks and the faint hum of artificial sunlight tubes.

Except now there was no sound at all.

The systems were still powered. The lights glowed with their soft yellow hue. The pumps worked. But the noise was gone — like the air itself had forgotten how to carry it.

And in the center of it all...

Rhea's body sat upright in one of the cultivation chairs. Eyes wide. Lips parted.

No signs of trauma.

No blood.

No defense wounds.

Except—

Her ears were missing.

Clean. Surgical. As if unstitched from the world.

And something had been written behind her eyes — so faint it could only be seen with UV light.

Three words.

"SHE HEARD IT."

Lar arrived first.

He stood there for five full minutes before calling it in.

Not frozen in fear. Not confusion.

He was listening.

To nothing.

"Where's the noise?" he finally asked Olivia.

She looked at him strangely.
"Noise?"

"The chamber. The tanks. They're silent."

"They've always made noise."

"I know."

She knelt near Rhea's body, examining the blank expression.
Still warm. No defensive marks. No signs of struggle.
Olivia looked up.
"How do you kill someone this way?"

"You don't," Lar said, his voice distant. "You turn them off."

Once again, Lar had no alibi.
He claimed he was asleep in the eastern corridor.
The logs showed no one there.
The camera?
Offline. "Glitch," he said.
But Olivia had manually calibrated that camera yesterday.

And when she checked the magnetic footprint in the corridor's flooring...

Lar's boots were the only pair recorded between 0200 and 0400.

Rhea died in 0311.

When she confronted him, his response was worse than denial.

"You think I did this?" he asked, and then laughed once, dry and hoarse. "I'm not sure I didn't."

"Lar..."

> "I've been waking up mid-step. I found blood under my nails. I don't remember dreaming, Olivia. That's not normal."

"You think you're possessed?"

"No. I think someone's writing through me."

Later that night, as Olivia tried to review Rhea's personal audio logs, she stumbled across an anomaly.

A corrupted recording.

Only six seconds of clarity:

> "It whispered from the lights. Not words. Just meaning... like something crawled into my head wearing a voice it hadn't earned."

Then silence.

Then one last line, clear and untouched:
> "Elias is listening through Lar."

Alone in his room, Lar tried to sleep.
He couldn't.
He couldn't even lie still.
His body twitched. His hands opened and closed.
He whispered to himself, not knowing the words.
And then, as he turned his head to the side, he saw it:
The mirror panel on the wall — hairline cracked from pressure — rippled.
Not cracked like glass.
Rippling. Like water.
And in the reflection, he saw his own body asleep on the bed.
But he was still standing.
Watching.
And behind him... something moved with his shadow, but not like it.
As though his shadow was being puppeted.

Sol 39
It began with a temperature drop.
A subtle dip of two degrees Celsius on the lower levels of Sector C — enough to be flagged, but not enough to trigger emergency systems.
Lar dismissed it at first. Olivia didn't.
She followed the duct trail manually, crawling through the service shaft. Her comms crackled, then died entirely

once she passed the fourth junction.

That should've been her first warning.

Her flashlight flickered.

And then she saw it: a wall that shouldn't be there.

But it wasn't just that. It wasn't on the internal scan either. It reflected nothing. Even her own shadow curved around it unnaturally, like light wanted no part of it.

"Lar... I think I found something," she whispered, knowing full well he couldn't hear her.

She pressed a gloved hand to the cold surface.

The metal hummed back.

She found an indentation—just enough to pry into. A hidden hatch. No buttons. No ID scanner.

No marks at all.

Only a seam.

She hesitated. Something about it felt wrong. Like it wasn't locked to keep people out.

It was locked to keep something in.

Still, Olivia forced it open.

The air hissed.

But not like decompression.

More like a long sigh.

The room was small. No larger than a shipping container. But the moment she stepped inside, her head swam — a wave of dizziness crashing over her as if she'd suddenly been submerged.

She steadied herself on the nearest wall.

That's when she saw the scratches.

Fingernail-deep gouges along every surface. They weren't random. They were patterns. Circles. Spirals. Overlapping eye shapes. A language not meant to be read.

On the far wall was a chair.

Bolted down.

With restraints.

Still closed.

Still stained.

And above it?

A camera.

But it wasn't theirs.

It was old. Dust-caked. Analog. Martian dust sealed in its seams.

Olivia's breath caught.

She turned to leave.

But before she could take a step...

A voice played over a nearby speaker.

Crackling. Genderless.

"Return to the chair. You were doing so well."

She froze.

The light flick.

Sol 39, 03:42 AM

The hatch hissed behind her.

Olivia froze, a cold sweat dripping under her collar. The room sealed without a sound, but she felt the air change — heavier now, like breathing against water.

No comms. No sound.

Just the soft ticking of unseen machinery.

And the chair.

It stood like a throne for the condemned: ancient, bolted, worn down by time and pain. The restraints were frayed but stained with a darkness that had soaked deep into the fibers. Blood. Old. Crusted. Human.

Too much for one person.

She wasn't alone in here.

Not anymore.

The speaker crackled.

"Return to the chair. You were doing so well."

Her chest tightened. The voice wasn't just sound — it was pressure, like someone pressing into her skull from inside.

She backed toward the wall. Her fingers brushed a groove in the metal — carved deep, looping over itself dozens of times.

It wasn't random.

It was words. Overwritten again and again in the same spot until the wall buckled slightly.

She traced them by touch:

"REMEMBER WHEN YOU ASKED FOR THIS."

Her knees weakened.

Lar stared at the monitor in disbelief. Static pulsed in waves, occasionally flickering back to show that room again. Olivia. The chair.

The blood.
He gripped the console.
"What the hell is this?"

The feed cut again, and another camera came online —
one he didn't know existed. This one showed a room full of
crew photos ,Not from their team.
Older ones.
Black-and-white. Worn faces. Smiling too wide. Tags
labeled "Mission Ares-3." "Phase Zero." "Subject Control
Alpha."
One photograph near the bottom had been scratched
out — violently.
Just one word remained visible beneath the smear:
LAR.

He recoiled.
"No. No, that's impossible. I wasn't—I didn't—"

But he couldn't finish the thought.
Because he recognized the room.
It was where Olivia was trapped now.
And somehow, some part of him knew...
It wasn't the first time he'd seen it.

Something was whispering.
Not from the walls. Not from the speaker.
From behind her eyes.

It murmured names she didn't remember. Numbers. Repeated patterns.

At the edge of her vision, the room twisted subtly — straight lines bending as though the corners had begun to peel into something else.

Then she saw them.

Faint fingerprints across the floor.

Not just hands.

Knees. Feet. Elbows. Heads.

The indentations of a hundred people, pressed into the floor like something beneath it had been trying to rise through human flesh.

And above it all, the only writing on the ceiling — traced by something that dripped upward:

"NO ONE LEAVES CLEAN."

Suddenly, the light went out.

A black so complete she couldn't tell if her eyes were open.

She backed against the wall, heart pounding — and then she heard something shift.

Wet.

Slow.

Alive.

Coming from the chair.

As he sprinted through the lower corridor toward Sector C, Lar began to hear voices.

But not in the hallway.

In the walls.

They moved with him. Echoed inside the pipes. Inverted voices — played backward — but he understood them.

They didn't want Olivia.

They wanted him.

"Come back to the chair."

"We missed you."

"You were almost complete."

His breath came in ragged gasps. He rounded a corner—and stopped.

The hatch to the hidden room was sealed shut.

No manual override.

His fingers trembled against the surface.

It was breathing.

And in the metallic sheen, his reflection looked at him...

...and winked.

Light snapped back on for Olivia.

But the room had changed.

Everything was mirrored — perfectly. Left and right reversed. Even her own movements.

Across from her now stood a replica of herself.

But it didn't move when she did.

It only smiled.

Then, it whispered:

"You're the copy, Olivia. I'm what came before."

And as Olivia backed away, her mirror self stepped forward—

real.

Solid.

Its smile widened. And it whispered, in a voice that sounded suspiciously like Elias:

"Get back in the chair. He's watching."

Sol 40

The morning came with a sick, artificial glow.

Jonas hadn't slept.

He'd stayed up in the command deck, poring over a backup cache from the auxiliary systems. It was buried behind four layers of corrupted architecture—non-indexed files never meant to be opened.

But they were there.

Audio logs. Diagnostic scans. Images.

And one folder.

PROJECT_MNEMOSYNE

He clicked it open.

The files were partially corrupted, as if something had chewed through the data—not time, but intent. Something didn't want them to be seen.

But some remained.

Enough.

Flickering footage.

A narrow room. Familiar. The same room Olivia had been trapped in.

In the center: a man strapped to the chair, twitching violently. His mouth moved, but the sound had been muted, or perhaps erased.

A timestamp from 23 years ago. Long before their colony's founding.

Suddenly, the footage cuts.

Now the man is calm. His eyes are open but all black. No irises. No whites.

A gloved hand enters the frame and places a mirror in front of him.

He smiles.

Then says—without sound—"It's still me, but closer to them."

"Subject response to stimulus has reached Stage 4. Self-awareness split confirmed. Host identity fully overwritten. Mnemosyne protocol succeeded... though the personality housed now is not the one we initiated. It mimics human memory with convincing clarity, but shows no emotional recall. It knows but it does not feel."

"This is not just memory reconstruction. It is replication. And replication... distorts."

"Termination of Subject 9 recommended. Refused by Overwatch."

"They want to see if it dreams."

Jonas's fingers trembled.
It wasn't just memory tampering.
It was an implantation.

Something about this room—its electromagnetic field, its isolation, its looping feedback of psychological input—had been used to rewrite people.

Memories weren't deleted.

They were replaced.

Over and over again.

Until the subject no longer knew what was real.

Until they believed they'd always been someone else.

And the worst part?

Jonas found his own name in the subject logs.

Twice.

Two different entries.

Two different personalities.

One marked INACTIVE. The other...

CURRENTLY ACTIVE.

As Jonas stepped back from the console, something drifted on the recycled air: the faint, sweet scent of burnt plastic.

It was coming from the ventilation system.

He followed it, knees shaking, crawling toward the smell.

Inside the duct, wedged into the grating like a warning, he found a blackened tape recorder. Melted. Half its casing fused.

But the tape inside?

Intact.

He played it back.

A voice. Female. Tired. Hollow.

"I'm Olivia. I think. I remember being Olivia. But I also remember watching her die. And I don't know if I'm the one who screamed... or the one who smiled."

"We're not clones. We're not people. We're echoes made solid."

"And something in that room is still recording us."

Click.
End of tape.

Jonas stumbled back, knocking over a chair. He collapsed, crawling backwards from the vent, his heart racing.

He remembered something—a dream he had every night but never told anyone.

A dream where he was strapped to that chair, and a woman in a silver suit whispered:

"Let's try again, Jonas. You'll like this one better."

And every time he woke up, he was crying.
But he never remembered why.
Until now.
He looked down at his hand.
And realized—
It was shaking like it belonged to someone else.

Sol 40, Evening

The light in the room had stopped flickering.

It had stabilized into a sick, warm orange — the exact hue of sunset on Earth. Not Mars. Earth. Olivia was certain of that.

She hadn't seen a real Earth sunset in over a year.

But this wasn't real.

This room had no windows.

She sat in the corner, arms wrapped around her knees, eyes locked on the chair in the center of the room like it might move if she blinked.

And the worst part?

It didn't frighten her anymore.

It felt like... home.

She didn't remember falling asleep. But she opened her eyes and the mirror across the room was no longer cracked.

It was perfect now. Polished. Flat like water.

And her reflection didn't mimic her movements.

It tilted its head in the opposite direction, eyes hollow and smiling too soon.

"You're remembering backwards, Olivia."

Her throat tightened.

"You were made to believe you were her. And you did so well. You were her. For a while."

The reflection blinked, slowly.

"But you never asked who she was before she was you."

Olivia clutched her temples.

The headache was like liquid static pouring into her skull. It buzzed and writhed — images swimming through her brain like slides in an old projector.

A different crew.

A different chair.

A woman sobbing while holding her own ID badge.

A name: Marla Hensley.

A flash of surgical lights.

Screaming behind mirrored glass.

And a question:

"Do you want to forget again?"

Her eyes widened.

That wasn't a memory.

It was a choice.

A file suddenly appeared on the monitor across the room — flickering to life on its own.

Project Mnemosyne: Subject ID #012-A. Designation: "Olivia Kerr."

It was a psych eval. Scanned, time-stamped, approved.

Dated 14 years ago.

Fourteen.

The real Olivia Kerr had been here before. A different team. A different experiment.

And this version of her — this Olivia — wasn't born.

She was installed.

Like software.
Carefully calibrated.
Made to believe.
She shook, cold down to the marrow, whispering to herself:
"That's not me. I'm real. I'm real. I remember my parents—"

But the more she said it, the more she realized those memories were vague.
Too clean.
Too structured.
Nothing lived in the in-between. No smells. No real noise. No flaws.
Like someone had edited them for maximum comfort.

A whisper trickled from the duct above.
Not Elias. Not Jonas. Not Lar.
Herself.
"You were the good version. The one that didn't scream too much."

"You almost passed."

"But now that you're remembering... it has to start again."

The chair creaked.
Empty.
Still, it creaked.
She turned her head — slowly — and saw a shadow cast on the wall behind the chair.
A human shadow.
Standing.
Watching her.
But no one was there.

She stood.
Backed away from the shadow. Her body shook uncontrollably.
In the mirror, her reflection stepped forward and spoke with a voice that layered over hers like two tracks played simultaneously:
"You were her once. Now you're you. But soon... you'll be someone new again."

She raised her hand to the mirror.
And this time, the glass felt warm. Soft. Like skin.

From outside the sealed chamber, Lar had returned.
He worked silently at the hatch.
"Olivia, it's me," he called through the door. "I think I can get it open."

Inside, she blinked. The mirror returned to being just glass.
The room was quiet again.

The chair no longer had blood on it.
But her hands did.
And she had no idea why.

Sol 40, Evening
The light in the room had stopped flickering.
It had stabilized into a sick, warm orange — the exact hue of sunset on Earth. Not Mars. Earth. Olivia was certain of that.
She hadn't seen a real Earth sunset in over a year.
But this wasn't real.
This room had no windows.
She sat in the corner, arms wrapped around her knees, eyes locked on the chair in the center of the room like it might move if she blinked.
And the worst part?
It didn't frighten her anymore.
It felt like... home.

She didn't remember falling asleep. But she opened her eyes and the mirror across the room was no longer cracked.
It was perfect now. Polished. Flat like water.
And her reflection didn't mimic her movements.
It tilted its head in the opposite direction, eyes hollow and smiling too soon.
"You're remembering backwards, Olivia."

Her throat tightened.
"You were made to believe you were her. And you did so well. You were her. For a while."

The reflection blinked, slowly.
"But you never asked who she was before she was you."

Olivia clutched her temples.
The headache was like liquid static pouring into her skull. It buzzed and writhed — images swimming through her brain like slides in an old projector.
A different crew.
A different chair.
A woman sobbing while holding her own ID badge.
A name: Marla Hensley.
A flash of surgical lights.
Screaming behind mirrored glass.

And a question:
"Do you want to forget again?"

Her eyes widened.
That wasn't a memory.
It was a choice.

—

A file suddenly appeared on the monitor across the room — flickering to life on its own.
Project Mnemosyne: Subject ID #012-A. Designation: "Olivia Kerr."
It was a psych eval. Scanned, time-stamped, approved.
Dated 14 years ago.
Fourteen.

The real Olivia Kerr had been here before. A different team. A different experiment.

And this version of her — this Olivia — wasn't born.

She was installed.

Like software.

Carefully calibrated.

Made to believe.

She shook, cold down to the marrow, whispering to herself:

"That's not me. I'm real. I'm real. I remember my parents—"

But the more she said it, the more she realized those memories were vague.

Too clean.

Too structured.

Nothing lived in the in-between. No smells. No real noise. No flaws.

Like someone had edited them for maximum comfort.

A whisper trickled from the duct above.

Not Elias. Not Jonas. Not Lar.

Herself.

"You were the good version. The one that didn't scream too much."

"You almost passed."

"But now that you're remembering... it has to start again."

The chair creaked.
Empty.
Still, it creaked.
She turned her head — slowly — and saw a shadow cast on the wall behind the chair.
A human shadow.
Standing.
Watching her.
But no one was there.
She stood.
Backed away from the shadow. Her body shook uncontrollably.
In the mirror, her reflection stepped forward and spoke with a voice that layered over hers like two tracks played simultaneously:
"You were her once. Now you're you. But soon... you'll be someone new again."

She raised her hand to the mirror.
And this time, the glass felt warm. Soft. Like skin.

From outside the sealed chamber, Lar had returned.
He worked silently at the hatch.
"Olivia, it's me," he called through the door. "I think I can get it open."

Inside, she blinked. The mirror returned to being just glass.

The room was quiet again.

The chair no longer had blood on it.

But her hands did.

And she had no idea why.

Sol 40, 21:18

The panel finally gave way with a sharp pop and a scream of stressed metal. Lar flung the door open, flashlight cutting through the thick, golden light within.

The first thing he saw was the chair.

Empty.

The second was Olivia, standing silently in the far corner, head turned slightly toward the mirror... which cracked down the center the instant the light hit it.

He stepped inside, slow, careful.

"Olivia?"

"Don't touch me."

Her voice was too calm. Like she was talking through someone else's mouth.

"What did you see in here?" he asked.

She didn't blink.

"I don't know. But it saw me first."

Olivia didn't speak on the way back.

Lar led her through the hallway like someone guiding a survivor out of wreckage, only the wreckage wasn't physical—it was her mind.

The others were waiting.

Jonas. Mira. Elias still missing.

And now Olivia's return brought no relief.

Only more questions.

"She doesn't look the same," Mira whispered.

"She's exhausted," Lar snapped. "She's been locked in a sealed room. Give her some—"

"No," Jonas interrupted quietly, his eyes sharp. "She's not exhausted. She's rewriting."

That word. That awful word again.

Olivia looked at him. And for a split second, Jonas flinched.

Because she looked at him like she didn't recognize him.

And worse—like maybe she used to.

They gave her water.

She didn't drink it.

Something in her gut whispered: not real. This taste isn't from memory. The brain can only simulate what it remembers.

And she didn't remember water tasting like this.

She looked around the group.

Mira had a small scar above her eyebrow. Olivia didn't remember that being there before.

> Jonas was wearing a different patch on his uniform—the Phase One logo, not the current Mars emblem.

Lar... Lar still looked the same.

And that's what frightened her the most.

Later that night, Lar found her in the empty greenhouse module, staring at the hydroponics.
"You said the room saw you."

She didn't look at him.
"It remembered me. Not like I'm remembering it. It was different. Like it knew I'd be back. Like I never left."

He sat beside her.
"We're all unraveling."

She laughed softly, eyes glassy.
"You still think this is unraveling? I think this is remembering."

Lar leaned in, whispering:
"Then tell me the truth. Do you think you're really Olivia Kerr?"

She turned to him, smile cold.
"Do you think you're really Lar?"

The silence between them was no longer comfortable. It was surgical.

From a distant hall monitor, Jonas watched the two of them sit together.
He turned off the audio. He didn't need it.
He zoomed in on Olivia's face.
She looked like Olivia.
Spoke like Olivia.
But in the shadow of her cheek, for just a flicker of one frame...
...her face didn't match.

Like it was something wearing her.
He paused the screen.
And behind her—reflected faintly in the greenhouse window—stood Elias.
Just for one frame.
Smiling.

89

CHAPTER VIII

The Footage That Watches

Sol 42

The storm outside had cleared.

No flickering lights. No whispered voices. No hidden rooms or mirrored horrors.

Just silence.

The kind that felt too normal, after everything.

The group was down to six: Olivia, Jonas, Lar, Mira, Renna, and Elias — though no one really trusted Elias anymore. No one knew where he'd been. And no one had any proof.

But for the first time in days, nothing happened.

No screams. No bodies.

It was almost worse than the murders.

Because now... they had to look at each other.

And wonder.

Who did this?

Lar led the charge.

He disconnected the corrupted camera network. Rebuilt a clean visual relay system. He insisted they reset logs. No more chasing ghosts or old files. From now on, only what they could see and verify counted.

Jonas agreed — reluctantly.

They even reassembled a crude central map of everyone's last known locations during each death. The patterns were vague.

Except one thing:

Each murder occurred when one specific person was "missing" or unaccounted for.

But that person changed.

First Elias. Then Olivia. Then Mira.

Now no one could claim innocence.

Elias gave a new version of where he'd been.

This time, he claimed he'd taken shelter in the outer thermal station during the comms collapse. Said he tried returning days ago, but the interior had changed.

Lar called him out.

"You told me it was because I wasn't remembering right. Now you say the base moved?"

Elias just smiled, too tired to fight. Or too calculating.

Olivia watched them all and realized:

We don't need ghosts anymore. We're doing this to ourselves now.

The voices were gone.

So were the hallucinations.

She was sleeping again. Eating. Holding a conversation without feeling split in half.

But now came something worse:

Guilt.

Memory.

Clarity.

And with it, one terrifying thought:

What if the killer is one of us—and always was?

What if the delusions had just masked that truth?

And now, reality was finally back.

Which meant the danger was finally real again.

Renna began keeping her own log. Separate. Offline. Paper.

Mira stopped sleeping near the group.

Jonas began locking himself in the main control room at night.

They didn't speak much anymore.

But when they did, it was always sharp. Loaded.

"Where were you during Sol 38?"

"Did you see her go into that corridor?"

"How long was the power out before you came back?"

The real horror was no longer the base.

It was the five other people in the room.

And the knowledge that only one of them had to lie for the rest to die.

Sol 43

The six of them stayed in the same room all night.

Lar's idea.

No one was to leave. No bathroom breaks alone. No isolation. No "malfunctions" in the dark. They would sleep in shifts. One person awake, watching. Everyone else accounted for.

It was paranoid.

It was humiliating.

It was necessary.

They chose the solar operations room, the only space with working locks on all doors and a reinforced window to the surface. They dragged in rations. Even a portable comm panel.

They would wait out the fear.

And prove none of them were killers.

Until one of them died.

Renna took first watch.

Then Jonas.

Then Mira.

Then Lar.

Then Olivia.

Then Elias.

Each took exactly two hours. Lar watched them start and end each shift. Every handoff was logged on his pad. No exceptions.

No one left.

And still, when the lights came up at Solrise—

Mira was dead.

Her eyes were open. Bloodless. Her mouth twisted, stretched unnaturally wide as if she'd been forced to smile.

There was no blood, no visible wound.

But something was missing:

Her tongue.

Gone.

Completely removed.

Olivia backed into the corner and vomited.

Lar staggered over to her side, hand trembling.

"No one left the room," Jonas whispered, cold sweat on his forehead. "No one."

"You don't know that," Renna hissed. "You fell asleep during Mira's shift!"

"No, I didn't! I remember—"

"Do you? Do you?!"

The comms were still running.
The logs were clear.
The cameras were on.
Lar rewound the footage himself.
They watched it.
Over and over.
There was Mira, lying still in her sleeping bag.
There was everyone else.
No one moved.
No one.
Even when her body jerked once in the dark.
Even when she stopped breathing.
Even when a faint, wet, slicing sound echoed faintly beneath the mic range.
Not a single person stirred.
Olivia sobbed silently.
"This isn't real. It's not real footage. This was edited—has to be—"

"By who?!" Jonas snapped. "Who the hell is smart enough to edit a live feed while they're sleeping? Lar double encrypted that line!"

They turned to Elias.

But Elias looked more horrified than any of them.

"You're all looking for a monster," he said quietly. "But what if it's not a monster anymore?"

"What does that mean?" Renna hissed.

"It means," Elias said, standing up, "that maybe one of you learned to kill in silence."

They buried Mira outside the base, under the red sand. No words. No ceremony. Just a tarp and a shallow grave in the cold Martian wind.

Afterward, no one returned to the same room.

They couldn't.

Instead, they split into pairs—Olivia with Lar, Jonas with Renna, Elias sleeping near the greenhouse door with a wrench under his pillow.

But they all knew the truth:

The killer was in the room.

They all watched the murder.

And none of them moved.

Sol 44, 03:12

Renna didn't sleep.

She hadn't slept properly in days, but tonight was different.

Tonight, she had a plan.

She waited until Jonas's breathing evened out — deep, measured, just past restless. They'd chosen the AI systems room, full of shadowy wiring and server cores still humming faintly under backup power. Jonas had taken the first shift. She'd offered second. He agreed.

That was his mistake.

She never intended to wake him.

Not tonight.

Renna had once overseen genetic contamination protocols for deep-surface sampling. She knew the process inside out: how trace particles from fingertips, nails, hair, skin oils — even moisture in breath — could be isolated.

If the killer touched Mira, she thought, they left something behind.

And there was one thing left that no one had noticed.

Mira's sleeping bag.

Folded hastily. Jammed into a supply crate outside.

Forgotten.

Renna slipped past the common corridor barefoot, gloves on, hair tied tight. No loose strands. She'd left a portable collector charging under her bunk for days, buried in a mess of blankets and heat packs.

Now it blinked green.

Ready.

She unzipped the sleeping bag, careful not to dislodge the fibers. The smell hit her immediately — stale sweat, iron, something unnatural — but she kept her hand steady.

The scanner purred softly as it passed over the inner lining.

It lit up once.

Then twice.

Then again — near the edge.

A dark stain. Almost invisible. At first glance, just another patch of faded fabric.

But under the UV wand, it gleamed faintly purple.

Not blood.

Not fluid.

Saliva.

Someone had leaned close. Close enough to breathe into her mouth. Close enough to tear out a tongue.

Renna gagged — then steadied herself.

"It's proof," she whispered.

She labeled the swab silently: MIRA_2443_SAL01

Placed it in the kit beside the others she'd gathered secretly over the past two days:

Jonas's food wrapper.

Elias's nail file.

Olivia's toothbrush.

Lar's gloves, with flaked callus skin near the palms.

One of you did it.

She didn't care about catching them for justice.
She wanted to know who to kill next if she had to.

A sound behind her — soft. Just a shift of pressure. Jonas murmuring in sleep.
But Renna froze.
Did he wake?

She turned, light off, data pad folded against her side. She slid silently back to the room.
Jonas hadn't moved. His eyes were still closed.
But his position had changed.
His arm had been across his chest earlier.
Now it was under the pillow.
Like he'd hidden something.
Like he'd been watching her.

She lay back down.
Eyes open.
Breathing slow.
Hands under her blanket, tightly clutching the DNA kit pressed against her ribs.
He might know.

But he doesn't know I know.

And if Renna had learned one thing about killers, it was this:
The moment they think you know, they don't hesitate.

So she wouldn't either.

Sol 45, 01:46

The bio-lab hadn't been used in days. The hydroponics had withered. Dust drifted in the recycled air like dandelion spores.

Renna entered silently, clutching her sample kit like it was sacred. The door clicked shut behind her — magnetically sealed. She manually disabled the entry log, a trick she remembered from her technician training. No one would know she'd been here.

She stood in the sterile dark, the only light from the small glow strip beneath the centrifuge. The machines still worked, but they were old. Slow. Prone to noise.

That was the risk.

Just two samples, she thought. Mira's stain. Elias's swab. If I can match epithelial or mitochondrial DNA, just one match, it'll be enough.

Not for court. But enough to act.
To survive.

She worked fast.

Pulled on gloves. Sanitized the table. Inserted the first swab into the thermal reader. It hissed faintly, scanning for viable cells.

Mira's sleeping bag sample was partially degraded, but still viable. The machine beeped once — processing.

She inserted Elias's in the second reader.

Then she waited.

Every second stretched.

Her breath fogged the inside of her mask.

She glanced toward the door. Still locked. Still no sign of movement. The vents above her let out a soft, repetitive pulse of air.

Like breathing.

A click.

Somewhere beyond the wall.

Renna froze.

The centrifuge spun slower now — nearing the match sequence. The screen flickered.

Don't crash. Please don't crash.

Another click.

A faint drag across metal.

She turned, ears sharp. Nothing moved in the lab. No shadows. No alerts.

But she could swear—

Was the storage locker... open?

She hadn't opened it.

She was sure.

The machine beeped.

She jumped.

One of the screens blinked:

> PARTIAL MATCH DETECTED. 61% MITOCHONDRIAL MATCH. POSSIBLE SECONDARY CONTAMINATION.

Renna blinked.
61%?

It wasn't full confirmation. But it wasn't nothing.
Either Elias had touched Mira just hours before her death...
Or someone planted his DNA.
And then the centrifuge screen flickered, a burst of static slicing through the image.
She backed away.
"No. No no no, not now—"

The lab lights died.
Pitch black.
And in the darkness, she heard it:
Breathing.
Not mechanical. Not vent pressure.
A real breath. Right behind her.

She didn't scream.
She just ran.
Fumbled toward the emergency exit. Hit the override.
Light burst through as the backup fluorescents kicked in.
There was no one behind her.
Just rows of metal counters.

But the storage locker was now wide open — and inside, hanging neatly like a ritual offering:

Mira's uniform.

Folded. Clean. Dry.

And underneath it — Elias's missing boots, caked with dust, as if someone had just taken them off after a long walk through the halls.

Renna yanked her samples from the centrifuge, jammed them into her pack.

She wiped the screens. Sprayed the airlock sensors. Cleared the boot logs.

She knew someone had been there with her.

She didn't know if it was Elias.

But whoever it was — they had walked into a locked lab, hidden in a locker, and vanished without a trace.

There's no logic here anymore, she thought.

Only lies dressed in evidence.

She left the bio-lab with one hand on her knife and the other over her heartbeat, whispering too fast to calm down.

"Sixty-one percent... sixty-one..."

Sol 45, 04:50

Lar hadn't slept since Mira.

He told Olivia he was fine — that he'd just "close his eyes for a bit" — but every time he tried, he saw Mira's body again.

That frozen smile.

That awful stillness.

It didn't leave you. Not here.

He was sitting in the rec dome, staring through the cracked glass at the Martian horizon, when Olivia came in. She didn't say anything at first. Just sat next to him, her arms wrapped tightly around herself.

"She's lying," she finally said.

Lar didn't look at her. He didn't need to.

"Renna?"

Olivia nodded. "Something changed after Mira. She's always moving when she thinks no one's watching. She's avoiding sleep, hiding her tablet... and last night she had blood on her boot."

Lar turned now.

"Are you sure?"

"It was dried, small — maybe days old. But it wasn't there before. I check. I check, Lar. I have to."

She sounded like she was unraveling.

But Lar didn't think she was wrong.

That night, they followed Renna.

Lar set up a dummy camera loop in the east corridor — a trick from his time repairing drone telemetry. Olivia waited near the greenhouse, just outside the bio-lab.

Renna didn't make them wait long.

She slipped into the lab with her kit tucked tight under her arm.

She didn't turn on the main lights.

But through the cracks in the door, they saw her activate the centrifuge.

"She's testing something," Olivia whispered. "God, Lar... she's doing it behind our backs. What if—"

"Wait."

They watched her move like she was cleaning up a crime scene. Methodical. Sharp. But not afraid.

Calm.

Too calm.

When she left, they didn't follow.

They went in after her.

It stank.

Not like death. Worse.

Like antiseptic covering something rotting underneath.

The machine was still warm.

In the bin: a stained swab. Labeled.

Lar pulled it out.

"Mira_2443_SAL01," he read aloud. "She tested saliva."

Olivia turned pale. "From the body?"

"Or the bag. Either way... she's trying to cross-match."

He checked the memory buffer. She'd wiped it. Of course she had.

But Lar was better.

He reached for the emergency diagnostics, a backup log of error corrections. It didn't have full samples — but it recorded all timestamps and test pairings.

Elias's sample had been cross-tested.

Mira's was logged five minutes earlier.

Renna was running private forensics. Not sharing results. Not warning them.

"She suspects Elias," Lar muttered.

"Or she's trying to frame him," Olivia whispered. "And she's doing it quietly. That's what's wrong. Her hands were clean, Lar."

"What do you mean?"

"When we found Mira... Renna was crying. Holding her mouth. Gagging. But I checked her sleeves after — not a trace of blood. Nothing. Like she knew how not to get dirty."

Lar looked at her.
Something cold passed between them.

Later, Olivia sat alone, reviewing their logs. Her hands trembled slightly. She could feel the warped edges of her memory again. They'd been sharper before. Back on Sol 1. She remembered faces more clearly then. Conversations weren't full of echoes.

But now—

She saw Mira's death in her head.

Except she wasn't sure if she saw it as it happened.

Or in the footage.

Or if she just imagined it so vividly it became memory.

"What did you see?" she whispered to herself. "What did you see?"

Lar returned to their room hours later. He had something in his hand — a torn piece of cloth.

"This was under Renna's bunk," he said. "It's Mira's. Dried blood in the seam."

"So she's the killer."

"No," he said quietly. "She's not. Or... not the only one."

Olivia looked up sharply.

"What?"

"There were two footprints under the cot. And they weren't hers. One was bare. One was booted."

He tossed the cloth on the table.
"Someone watched her. While she hid the evidence. Someone helped."

They stared at the scrap of bloodstained fabric.
Then at each other.
And then — a sound across the hall.
A scream.
Not loud.
Just cut off.

Sol 45, 08:03
Renna hadn't slept again.
She sat on the floor of the unused communications room, knees pulled up to her chest, staring at the black mirror of the powered-down console.
They were watching her.

She didn't know who. But something had changed. The quiet glances. The moments when a conversation stopped as she entered. The faint echo of footsteps behind her that didn't match her rhythm.
You wanted to know who the killer was, Renna, she told herself.

What if it's you?

But that was ridiculous.

She hadn't killed anyone.

She'd only collected evidence. Studied behaviors. Quietly ensured her own survival while the others lost themselves to grief, madness, and suspicion.

And yet...

Her door had been ajar this morning.

She was certain she'd sealed it.

She checked the evidence kit hidden beneath the false panel in her locker.

It had been touched.

Not rifled through — no, whoever had opened it had been careful, methodical, just like her.

Someone had read the labels.

Someone knew she was watching.

She stared at the samples one by one. Mira. Elias. Olivia. Lar.

Her eyes lingered on Jonas.

She didn't remember collecting his.

But there it was: a fiber swab tagged from the mess hall vent — right where Ava had been found.

Did I take that?

Did someone plant it?

Or did I collect it and forget?

Her mind felt like glass — perfectly reflective, but full of hairline cracks.

Renna worked best in systems.
Biological ones. Chemical. Logical.
So she made a new chart.
Four columns. Five names. Six behaviors.
She gave each person a risk index based on psychological volatility, access to corpses, and past behavior anomalies.
Elias: erratic, disappeared for hours, possible murderer.
Jonas: quiet, observant, has military field training.
Lar: loyal, but too clean. Might be hiding something.
Olivia: frayed, highly intelligent, starting to doubt herself. Dangerous in an unpredictable way.
Renna's own name?

She left that column blank.
No one should self-diagnose. Bias.

She left the room at 09:17.
Just for food. Water. Movement.
When she returned ten minutes later...
Her door was locked.
The keypad had been reset.
She stood there, frozen, staring at the blinking red panel.

This time, she hadn't closed it.

Someone had gone inside — and sealed it behind them.

"Who's in there," she said softly.

No answer.

But she heard it.

A soft scrape inside. Like metal on tile.

Her hand hovered over the emergency override.

Then she stepped back.

She wasn't going to confront them.

Not yet.

She needed to know more.

"You want to play?" she whispered to the door.

"Fine. Let's play."

Renna moved fast.

She bypassed the airflow sensors on the lab door and disabled the bunk motion triggers. Then she went to the central console — still partially functional — and pulled up old security footage archives.

Someone had wiped segments.

But only around her quarters.

Who deletes data only around one person?

Only someone afraid of what it showed.

She found a corrupted log, timestamped 02:42.

Just a flash of static.

Then a blurred shape, leaning over her locker.

Just long enough to copy labels.

Then... a glint of something in their hand.

Not a weapon.
A mirror.

They weren't just watching her.
They were trying to make her doubt herself.
This was next-level gaslighting.
Confuse the scientist. Break her grip on logic. Make her seem unhinged.
But Renna wasn't breaking.

She was adapting.
They'd stolen her evidence?
She'd start again.
She had blood in the filtration system. Hair on the battery housing. Skin flakes in the helmet seals. This base was a cathedral of microscopic proof.
She'd gather it again.
She'd match every trace.
And when I find you, she thought, staring at the screen as the static looped endlessly...

...I won't need to prove it to the others.

I'll just take you apart quietly. Like a bad experiment.

Sol 45, 10:05
The scream was short.
Just one breath — as if someone had been startled, or caught mid-sentence, and then snuffed out like a flame.

Lar and Olivia froze in place, their ears straining into the sudden, icy quiet of the corridor.

"Med bay?" Olivia whispered.

Lar had already started moving.

They passed the northern passage — flickering light panels casting long, surreal shadows — and sprinted past the greenhouse dome. Each corridor felt darker than the last. The emergency power flickered now and then, casting the whole place in pulsing red light.

It didn't feel like a habitat anymore.

It felt like a trap.

They reached the med bay.

Empty.

But something was wrong.

The cot was overturned.

The IV stand, twisted and bent, leaned against the wall like it had been used to brace a fall.

"Who was here?" Lar hissed.

"Renna checked Ava's vitals here this morning."

Olivia crouched near the floor. A faint smear — blood, recently wiped, with cloth fibers tangled in it.

But Ava was gone.

No body.

No trail.

Just the echo of that scream, and a wet towel clumped in the sink — like someone had tried to clean something... fast.

"She's not here," Olivia said, her voice low.

"Yeah. But she was."

Lar turned, eyeing the far wall.
Then he saw it.
The panel to the maintenance shaft.
Slightly ajar.
The hinge was warped — someone had forced it open from the inside.

Lar climbed in first.
The metal creaked under his weight. The shaft was narrow, just enough space for crawling. Olivia followed, the two of them breathing heavily in the pitch-black dark.
About ten meters in, the shaft widened.
A storage grate had been popped.
And there, barely lit by the beam of Lar's wristlight, lay the trailing edge of a hospital gown.
"Ava..."

Olivia crawled forward — but Lar grabbed her wrist sharply.
"Wait."

She followed his gaze.

The gown was torn — but strategically arranged. As if someone wanted it found.

And underneath it...

Nothing.

No body. No blood.

Just the cold echo of empty ducts.

"They're playing with us," Lar whispered. "Like a breadcrumb trail."

"Why?" Olivia whispered.

"Because they want us to doubt. To panic. To split."

He scanned the narrow crawl space again.

Then froze.

Scratch marks.

On the walls. Tiny. Repeated. Like fingernails.

"Someone was dragged. Or clawed. Trying to hold on."

Olivia felt a sharp sting in her head.

A memory. Too sudden.

She saw Elias, hunched in a hallway days ago. His fingers bleeding. Muttering into the comms.

"Not here... not in the vents. Not again. She's still there."

But the memory warped — like it didn't belong to her.

She wasn't sure she had actually seen him do that. Or if someone had described it to her. Or if it was just something she thought she'd heard while dreaming.

"Lar... I don't know what's real anymore."

Her voice cracked.

"Every time we move forward, something resets. Something's always missing. I thought Renna was lying, but maybe she's right. Maybe we all are. Maybe someone's making sure we remember wrong."

Lar put a hand on her shoulder.

It was the first truly human gesture she'd felt in days.

"Then we write everything down. We say it out loud. We test each other. We stop letting our heads be the only place the truth lives."

"What if we've already lost it?"

He didn't answer.

They backed out of the shaft, found themselves in the far wing locker room.

And there — as the overhead lights flickered on — they found something worse than a body.

A mirror.

Standing. Not mounted. Freestanding. Oval-shaped. Polished clean.

It hadn't been there before.

Someone had dragged it in.

Carved into the surface — shallowly, with something sharp — were the words:

"I KNOW WHO YOU ARE."

Lar stepped forward slowly, reaching out to brush the surface — and recoiled.

The mirror was warm.

"Where's Elias?" Olivia whispered.

They regrouped. Pulled Renna into a private corridor. Confronted her about Ava's disappearance.

She didn't blink.

"What would you like me to say?" Renna said, coolly. "That I killed her? That I stuffed her into the vent after carving a message on a mirror in cursive?"

"Do you know where she is?" Olivia asked, her voice rising.

Renna leaned in.

"No. But I think I know who does."

Lar tensed. "Who?"

Renna stared at both of them.

And smiled.

"The person who hasn't spoken since the scream."

CHAPTER IX

The Silent Variable

Sol 45, 10:10

Jonas had stopped reacting to screams.

They came too often now — in reality, in dreams, in half-waking states where corridors pulsed red and shadows moved without bodies. If you chased every sound in this place, you ended up dead or mad.

So instead, he listened.

And waited.

And recorded.

He'd been spending most of his time in the old engineering substation, two levels down. The others thought it had been sealed due to a CO_2 leak. It hadn't. Jonas had sabotaged the detectors himself.

He needed somewhere clean — somewhere untouched by the chaos, where he could sift through what no one else had the clarity to see.

On one wall he had taped photos: stills from security footage, fragments Renna had missed, timestamps that didn't match up. He had audio logs — distorted, manipulated, some spliced mid-sentence — but others... others were raw.

There were voices there.

Multiple voices, sometimes layered over each other. Always around moments of death.

Once, during Elias's disappearance, Jonas had played one back at full gain.

He heard three breaths.
Only two had names.

Jonas didn't believe in hauntings.
He believed in strategy.
And what was happening to them wasn't chaos — it was orchestration. Designed to break cohesion. Break memory. Break sanity.
The murders weren't random.
They happened at transition points — after discoveries. After doubts were voiced aloud.
Mira died after suggesting someone else had been on the base.
Dr. Lang died after refusing to let the body be moved.
Ava disappeared right after Renna started collecting DNA.
And now... Elias was missing.
"So the pattern is: truth equals punishment," Jonas whispered to the empty room.

He stared at the whiteboard again.
There were names circled.
One name in red.
Not because Jonas thought he was the killer — but because he needed to make sense of Lar.
Too clean. Too moral. Too ready to play the hero.

Is that how you survive a slaughter? Or how you get away with it?

There was one last thing Jonas hadn't shared.

A journal, found in the floor vent near storage wing six — beneath an old panel, taped in place.

Handwritten.

Not standard issue.

It wasn't his.

It wasn't Elias's.

It wasn't anyone's — not from this mission.

It dated back two years.

It described things no one had admitted to publicly — oxygen shortages, containment breaches, four unrecorded fatalities. It ended mid-sentence:

"...tried to warn them. The new team will find what we—"

Then the ink streaked off the page.

But Jonas checked all mission logs. All public archives.

There was no mention of a prior crew.

"Because there wasn't supposed to be one," he whispered.

But he didn't bring the journal to Lar. Or Olivia. Or Renna.

Because if it was fake — if someone had planted it — he needed to know why.

That's when he saw it.

In the reflection of the darkened console — movement, behind him.

A quick, insect-fast flicker of shadow, near the corridor door.

He turned.

Nothing.

"Show yourself," he said softly.

Silence.

But the door was open now.

He hadn't left it open.

He left the substation behind, sliding the journal into the folds of his jacket.

He would go above now.

Back into the red-lit world of fractured survivors and ticking paranoia.

He would act like one of them.

He would listen.

He would console.

He would nod when they accused each other.

And when the next body dropped, Jonas would be watching.

Because he was done reacting.

He was going hunting.

Sol 45, Approximate Time Unknown

Location: Sub-Level Utility Network – Unmapped Sector

Elias had stopped counting days. Or hours. Time meant nothing down here — beneath the base, between steel ribs and concrete organs. The pipes groaned like sleeping animals. Fluorescent lights buzzed overhead like hornets ready to swarm.

He wasn't hiding.

He was waiting.

And sometimes... listening.

Other times, he was talking.

But not to anyone.

"I'm still here," he whispered, knuckles brushing a cold wall.

"Still with you. I never left."

He didn't know who he was saying it to anymore. Mira? Dr. Lang? Himself?

Or maybe... someone who had never had a name.

He walked barefoot now. The boots had become too loud. Down here, silence meant safety. Still, sometimes the metal corridors whispered back when he walked. Words in steam. Words in clinks and echoes.

He'd seen his reflection move when he hadn't.

He'd seen doorways shift two feet to the left, only to return with no explanation.

And once, a woman with no face sat in the darkness, her hands bleeding into her lap.

She never spoke.

She only smiled.

He reached the old conduit chamber — the one no longer on any schematics.

This was where he remembered them dragging someone. A body.

"Lang," he muttered.

The smell still lingered: antiseptic and copper and something... burnt.

But there was no body now.

Only a red smear leading up the wall, then into the ventilation duct.

A trail made upward, as if the body had tried to climb out of gravity.

"No. No — I saw this," he whispered, turning in circles.

"This already happened. Or it's going to."

His fingers trembled.

He pressed his palms to the floor.

It was still warm.

Something had been here, minutes ago.

Watching.

He should never have taken the comms unit. But he had.

And now he carried it like a noose.

It buzzed at random intervals.

No voices. Just static.

Until once — just before sleep — he heard Lar's voice.

But twisted. Distorted. Slow.

"You're not alone. You never were. You brought it with you."

He smashed the unit against the wall.

It still buzzed.

Then Olivia's voice came through.

She wasn't speaking. She was screaming.

And then... Renna. Calm. Cold.
"We'll find you. We'll fix you."

The final chamber.
The mirror again.
The same one he'd broken in the mess hall days ago —
somehow down here now.
Uncracked.
Unsmiling.
He stepped toward it.
And saw himself, mouth moving... but no sound.
Behind his reflection, someone was standing.
Wearing Jonas's face.
But the eyes were empty.
No irises. Just black pits.
The figure didn't blink.
Didn't move.
Elias screamed, flinging the mirror down.
It shattered — but no sound came.
Not even the shattering.

He climbed, finally, back toward the main base.
No longer sure why.
Not to join them.
Not to warn.
Not even to kill.
He just wanted to know... what he still was.
As he crawled out of the lower shaft, he heard them.
Voices.
Real ones.
Olivia. Lar. Renna.
Whispers, distant, somewhere in the habitat.
But none said his name.

None seemed to realize... he was already back.

Already moving through the walls.

Sol 46, 07:12

Main Habitation Wing – Medical Station

The base's med-bay had once been bright and sterile, a place of certainty and protocol. Now it felt like a war zone's triage unit — stripped of resources, soaked in dread, and whisper-quiet.

That was where Grace lived now. Or more accurately — where she refused to leave.

She was the last standing doctor, and unlike everyone else, she didn't wander the halls whispering theories. She patched the living, buried the dead, and kept score of every unexplained trauma.

And now, Jonas stood just outside her sliding door, debating whether to knock.

"Don't hover," came a voice through the glass.

Jonas froze. Then slowly stepped inside.

Grace didn't look up right away. She was stitching something. Not a person — a piece of synthetic tissue. Practicing. Or distracting herself.

When she did look up, her eyes were sharp. Awake. Tired but intact.

"Jonas. Finally found time to get that arm looked at?"

He glanced down at the gash he'd ignored for days.

"Didn't notice."

"You will. Infection likes people who pretend to be invincible."

There was no fear in her tone. Just clean practicality — and something else. Steadying warmth, like she was keeping herself anchored by anchoring others.

She gestured to the cot. "Sit. Or stand. Just don't bleed on the notes."

Jonas sat.

He watched her work in silence as she cleaned the wound. No unnecessary chatter. No questions about who did it.

"You still trust any of us?" he asked after a while.

She paused. Then shrugged.

"I trust you're in pain. That's enough for today."

He almost smiled.

It wasn't flirtation. Wasn't tender. It was honest care — something he hadn't felt in weeks.

She finished the bandage, then leaned back on her stool and wiped her hands.

"You're not sleeping," she said.

"Neither are you."

"Difference is, I remember when I started losing sleep. You... I think you've forgotten how to rest."

He stared at her, something uneasy flickering in his chest. She was reading him. Not suspecting him — just seeing him. That was worse, somehow.

"I found a journal," he said quietly.

Her brow furrowed. "What kind?"

"One that says we're not the first crew here."

She didn't flinch.

"Then we dig. Carefully."

Not What? Not Are you sure?

Just solid ground, where everyone else had turned to shifting sand.

She handed him a water pouch. He hadn't realized how thirsty he was.

"You're not crazy, Jonas. Not yet."

"You don't know that."

"I know you're still checking. That's what matters."

For the first time in days, he nodded without suspicion.

They said nothing else for ten minutes. Just the soft hum of med-bay systems and the distant creaks of an unstable station.

When he finally left, he paused at the door.

"You ever think about what comes next?"

"Like surviving this?"

"Like what's left of us after we do."

She looked at him — really looked.

"Let's make it there first. Then I'll tell you what I see in you."

Sol 47, 03:08

Med-Bay, Lower Habitation Module

The base groaned with its own weight — like it, too, had begun to unravel under the tension.

Most of the crew were either asleep, hiding, or missing.

But Grace couldn't sleep. And Jonas had stopped pretending he ever did.

They met in silence again — him at her door, her already knowing he'd come.

She didn't ask why he was there.

He didn't explain.

It had become a ritual: Jonas arriving with some phantom injury, Grace offering care without comment. Tonight, it was his shoulder — bruised from slamming into a bulkhead while chasing... something that hadn't been there.

Or maybe had.

He sat shirtless, and she cleaned the skin carefully, her gloved fingers grazing just enough to remind him he was still human. Still here.

"You're shaking," she said gently.

"Am I?"

"Yes."

She didn't mention how close she sat. How her voice softened more with him than with anyone else. She didn't need to.

He let out a slow breath.
"Do you think we'll get off this rock?"

She didn't answer right away.
Then:
"Maybe. Maybe not."

"That's optimistic."

"No. That's honest. But I'm not planning on dying for this place."

She paused.
"I don't want you to either."

Jonas blinked. That was the first time anyone had said something like that to him since it all began — since Mira, since Lang, since Elias disappeared into whatever black corner of the base had swallowed him.
He looked at her — really looked.
"Why me?"

"Because you're trying. Because you haven't shut down. You're terrified, and I see it — but you're still here. That counts."

"What if I lose it next?"

She didn't look away.
"Then I'll remind you who you are."

Something stirred in his chest — not longing, exactly. Something older. Recognition.

The kind of pull you feel when someone sees you without flinching.

As she leaned in to bandage his shoulder, her hand hesitated.

She didn't move away.

Neither did he.

There was half an inch between their faces, both breathing shallow, not from fear but from a rising heat neither had expected.

Then a distant crash echoed — a vent collapsing somewhere above. A body? Or just the station sinking into itself again?

The moment passed.

But not before Jonas looked into her eyes and said:

"If we get through this... I want to see where this goes."

She didn't answer in words.

She just nodded — slowly, meaningfully.

And then she did something only Grace could have done in a place like this:

She reached out, rested her palm on his chest — just once, softly — and said:

"Don't break."

The lights flickered.

Overhead, the comms crackled.

But it wasn't Elias this time.

It was static. Then a click. Then a whisper:

"One of you... doesn't bleed right."

Grace stiffened.

Jonas stood.

All warmth vanished. The med-bay dimmed.

The horror was back.

But this time, they weren't facing it alone.

Sol 47, 23:41

Secure Storage Room – Admin Terminal Access (Subsection C-4)

The storage room had been sealed since the first incident. Originally used to house backup recordings and emergency logs, it was the kind of place no one thought to check anymore. Half the cameras were fried. The lights flickered in alternating amber and pale blue. The room smelled wrong—like mildew, melted plastic, and something else beneath it...

Decay.

But Olivia had the access code. Ava had given it to her weeks ago during a quiet lunch, scribbled on the corner of a nutritional wrapper.

"In case something happens to me," Ava had said, laughing softly. "Because let's be real. Something always does."

Now Ava was gone.

And Olivia had waited too long.

—

There were over 1,200 hours of recordings indexed under Ava's ID tag. Most were mundane. Crew diagnostics. Sleep cycle summaries. Medical flags. Some showed Jonas wandering the halls. Others showed Elias... just standing for hours, unmoving, staring into corners.

But then she found it.

A hidden subfolder labeled:

[DEVOURING // AVA PRIVATE // LOCKED MEMORY STREAM]

Her heart thudded.

The file was timestamped two days before Ava was found barely alive in the vent.

At first, the footage was nothing.

Just Ava in her private cabin. Quiet. Drinking tea. Watching the static flicker from a cracked wall panel. The lights behind her blinked out and came back on again — except they didn't match the room's true layout.

The footage looked... off. Wrong angles. Walls slightly misaligned. Like someone had recreated her room, but couldn't get it exactly right.

Ava blinked at the camera — then whispered:

"This isn't where I sleep. This is where it watches me sleep."

Olivia leaned forward.

The camera glitched.

Then Ava was no longer alone.

There was no entry sound. No door creak. But something had appeared in the footage behind Ava — not visible directly, only reflected in the wall's darkened display screen.

A man. Standing.

Not facing her.

Facing the wall.

Still.

Too still.

He was tall, gaunt, with shoulders sloped like they'd been broken and reset wrong. The reflection showed his mouth moving, but no audio played. The room's sound remained utterly silent.

Then Ava said:

"He doesn't live here. He remembers here."

And she smiled.

But her eyes were full of absolute terror.

Olivia tried to pause the footage.

It wouldn't stop.

The audio returned, faint, over layers of static:

"You came here to dig. So dig. But you don't like what's underneath."

"One of you brought it in your blood."

Ava's voice followed, frantic and off-screen:

"I saw them in the cryopod logs, Olivia! There were seventeen, not sixteen—there was another, but no face, no name—just an ID: ECH0-0-1—"

The screen blinked.

Then Ava was back, sitting on the floor, staring directly into the camera.

"I think it's inside one of us now."

The screen cut to static.

Then flashed briefly — a still image:

A frozen, blood-soaked interior shot of one of the cryo-chambers. The nameplate read:

GRACE HOLLAND. Status: Unknown. Arrival: 17 of 16.

Olivia backed away from the screen.

What was worse — the idea that Grace had lied?

Or that Grace hadn't arrived at all, but was already here when they woke up?

Or worse still: that someone else had come in using Grace's pod, and no one noticed?

Behind her, a quiet hiss.

She turned.

A mirror shard — from a maintenance bot panel — reflected something behind her...

Someone standing in the doorway.

But when she spun around — the room was empty.

The recording console shut itself down.

Sol 48, 04:29

Medical Bay – Personnel Terminal 03A – Grace Holland

Grace stared at her own login panel, heart pounding.

Five failed attempts.

That didn't make sense. She never forgot her credentials. Her hands hovered over the keypad, trembling. The silence around her was too thick — like the walls themselves were waiting.

She finally entered her old backdoor sequence — a holdover from her early days in med school.

It worked.

The system unlocked.

But what she saw twisted her stomach into ice:

LOG DATA – INCOMPLETE

PATIENT RECORDS: CORRUPTED

SECURITY PROTOCOL OVERRIDES: AUTHOR - HOLLAND.G

That last line made her blood run cold.

She hadn't overridden anything. She hadn't accessed the high-clearance sectors in days. But the logs said she had. Someone had used her ID. Or worse...

Someone was her.

Grace accessed her own neural trace data—a biometric scan they all wore on rotation.

The system flagged something immediately:

Time Unaccounted: 02:11:54 – Sol 46, 23:50 – Sol 47, 02:02

Reason: "Medical Sedation / Personal Consent"

She hadn't been sedated.
She hadn't given consent.
She had no memory of those two hours.
Her last recollection from that night was standing outside the lab, hearing whispers through the glass wall — and then waking up in her quarters, fully clothed, shoes still on, as if she'd never made it back properly.

Grace paced the bay.
No one else was around. Olivia, Lar, Jonas — all elsewhere. She couldn't tell who was still in their rooms or hiding in the air ducts like Renna had last said.
She opened a cabinet.
Empty.
Then another.
Nothing.
But in the third drawer, beneath sealed injectors and gauze, she found something that didn't belong:
A bloody surgical mask. Folded. Tucked. Still damp.
She recoiled — the inside stained with something black, not red. Not fully blood. Not normal.
Attached to it with medical tape:
CRYO ID: 17

Her ID.
The one Olivia had seen in the logs.

She turned to the vent — just in time to hear it.
A whisper.
So close, it should have been right beside her ear.

"She doesn't know what she is."

Grace dropped the mask.
Backed up.
"Who said that?" she called out, her voice shaking. "WHO'S THERE?!"

Silence.
Just the soft mechanical breathing of the base.
Then, from the terminal — a sound. A system booting.
The screen flickered, displaying one line:
"There were never sixteen. There was always one more."

And beneath it:
"DOCTOR GRACE HOLLAND // MISSION ENTRY LOG: REDACTED // FILE DATE: BEFORE LAUNCH"

For the first time since they arrived, Grace violated official protocol.
She walked out of the med bay without alerting command.
She didn't log her departure.
She didn't bring a medkit.
She brought only a scalpel, slid up her sleeve, and a single message hastily written in her notes folder, marked

PRIVATE:

If you find this, check pod seventeen. If it's empty — it's already too late.

As the hallway swallowed her into silence, a motion detector somewhere deep within the base flickered on.

Not because of her.

Because someone else was moving too.

CHAPTER X

The Fortgotten One

Sol 49 – 02:11

Interior – Lower Maintenance Level – Former Storage Sector 3D

The walls felt too close.

The air was still, unnaturally so — like it had been drained from the room moments before someone screamed.

Grace stood by the threshold of the old maintenance wing, heart racing. Her hand trembled over her comms. Lar was just behind her, flashlight flickering in the stale, recycled air.

"I thought this section was sealed," he whispered. "It was marked as compromised weeks ago."

"It is," Grace said. "But Renna said she saw someone come through here. She followed them."

She didn't finish that sentence. Renna never came back out.

Then they heard it — low, echoing, like a whimper tangled in metal:

> "I didn't mean to... I swear I didn't mean to."

A voice.
Familiar.
Olivia.

They found her crouched beside a rusted coolant pipe, legs pulled into her chest, face wet, her hands shaking uncontrollably. A dim blue emergency light from the floor flickered every ten seconds, casting her in pulses of shadow and sickly hue.

Olivia didn't look up.

She didn't acknowledge their presence at all — not until Grace touched her arm gently.

And then Olivia screamed.

Not in fear.

In guilt.

"Don't touch me! Don't—don't look at me!"

Lar stepped back, stunned.

Grace stayed kneeling.

"Olivia," she said softly. "You're safe. But you're scaring us. What happened down here?"

Olivia looked at her — and something in her eyes was broken.

"I did it."

"There was another. One of us. No one ever noticed he was gone."

Lar's face went pale. "Who?"

"I don't remember his name."

She wiped her mouth with the back of her sleeve, smeared with grease and blood. "He was part of the recon team. Quiet. Always alone. Kept to the service corridors, monitoring... soil readings. Cameras. I can't remember his face, Grace."

Her voice broke into a whisper.

"But I remember what he looked like when I killed him."

The silence hung for a long time.

No one spoke.

Not even Lar.

"I went down here a few weeks ago," Olivia whispered. "Late at night. I couldn't sleep. The corridors felt like they were calling me. And he was already down here. Sitting by the broken pressure valve, muttering..."

She swallowed.

"He said I wasn't real. That I was a copy. That I'd already died before launch."

"He tried to cut my arm. Said he could prove it. Said we were replacements."

Lar's jaw clenched.

Grace stared at Olivia in horror.

"I don't remember deciding to do it," Olivia said, voice barely audible. "I just remember the wrench. And the first hit. And how long it took him to stop moving."

She turned to them, slowly, eyes hollow.

"And then I forgot."

"I forgot him. I forgot what I did. Until tonight."

Grace didn't want to believe it. But something in Olivia's shaking hands told her this wasn't a psychotic break.

It was a return of memory.

A memory that had been violently scrubbed.

She and Lar followed Olivia deeper into the corridor. She pointed to a rusted panel behind an old generator vent.

"I stuffed him in there," she said. "I remember... breaking the seal... It was easier than it should've been."

Lar pulled it open.

Even before the light hit the cavity, the smell hit them.

Sweet rot. Decay mixed with coolant.

Inside: A body, curled unnaturally, legs bent backward, arms broken and pressed to the chest as if in prayer. The face was partially gone — decay or something else had eroded the features.

But he was wearing a Mars-issued suit.

His ID tag, half melted into his chest plate, read:

WATSON // GEOLOGICAL TECH-2

None of them remembered him.

Not even Grace, who had run psych evals on all sixteen members.

Not even Lar, who had overseen team logistics.

But now the truth was pressing through the floorboards like a pulse:

There had been a seventeenth.

Back in the corridor, Grace clutched the wall, trying to control her breathing.

How could they not have known?

How could no one remember him?

Lar finally said it:

"This... this wasn't Olivia's doing."

"Something's been rewriting our memories. Cleansing them. We're remembering in fragments because we weren't meant to remember at all."

He looked down the corridor again, where the shadows pulsed with strange rhythm.

"Something down here is hiding us from ourselves."

And Deeper Still...

As they began to head back up, Olivia halted. Her eyes widened. She pointed upward.

"The cameras," she whispered. "They're pointing at that wall."

There were no cameras visible.

But as they stared, the dim wall in front of them began to shimmer — just slightly. As if a layer of light was peeling away.

And behind it:

A small door.

Metallic. Seamless.

Not in the blueprints.

Olivia stepped forward. Then froze.

There, at the center of the door — scratched into the surface like it had been carved with nails:

"SEVENTEEN IS A LIE"

Sol 50 – 03:07

Interior – Medical Bay – Habitat Sector C

Grace awoke not from sleep, but from something closer to a blackout.

She didn't remember falling asleep at her desk, but her neck was stiff, her lab coat still on, and her data pad lay powered off in front of her. The glow of the overhead surgical lights was still on — a soft, sterile blue.

Her mouth was dry.

Something in the air felt... touched.

She stood slowly, brushing her fingertips across the desk. Her mug was cold. Her instruments slightly out of place. The chair at the secondary console had been moved exactly 6 inches to the right.

Grace was meticulous. She always left it centered.

"Computer," she called out, voice cracking, "Access Med Bay Log: last user activity."

A soft chime. Then:
Accessing...

Last login: Dr. Grace Howard // 01:48 – Biometric confirmation complete.

Data access: Gene sequencing files, crew DNA logs, cryo-recovery analytics.

Grace frowned.
That wasn't possible.
She had gone to bed around midnight after securing the lab. She hadn't come back down. She knew that.

"Playback security footage from 01:30 to 02:00," she said, now heart hammering.

There was a pause.
Error: Footage unavailable.

Footage has been manually erased.

She stood frozen in the sterile glow of the lab.
Someone had used her login. Her biometrics. Her identity.
And then deleted the evidence.
Grace walked slowly to the storage unit — the one where she kept DNA samples she'd been secretly gathering. One vial for each crew member. Including her own.
She had started the collection days ago. Quietly. Without official approval.
She entered the 12-digit passkey.
The drawer hissed open.
Four vials were gone.
Jonas. Olivia. Elias. Herself.
Only their names had been removed from the manifest — as if those samples had never existed.
She stumbled backward, nausea curling her gut. Her chest tightened with a creeping realization:
Someone knew she was testing. And someone had removed the evidence before she could act.
The Mirror
She rushed into the back room — where she kept the biometric scanner and facial recognition logs. A hidden

terminal. Not on the main med bay grid.

She flicked the screen on.

Last scan: 01:49 // IDENTIFIED: Dr. Grace Howard

But the image that loaded... wasn't her.

It was a woman who looked like her.

Same height. Same posture. Same lab coat.

But her eyes. The left one twitched unnaturally. Her smile was off, like it had been practiced in front of a mirror too many times.

Grace's hand shook violently as she reached for the console. The playback paused on the frozen image.

This wasn't an impersonation.

This was a duplicate.

Footsteps

Suddenly — the sound of footsteps outside the med bay.

Soft. Then pausing.

Then three soft taps on the frosted glass of the entrance.

She spun around, heart in her throat.

"Jonas?" she called out, breathless.

No answer.

The taps repeated.

Not knocks. Taps.

Deliberate. Even.

Grace backed away, hand on the scalpel drawer.

The door slid open.

No one was there.

Only a small, sealed container, resting perfectly in the center of the threshold.

Inside: a bloodied DNA vial. Her name written in black marker across the label — not typed.

Underneath, a small strip of paper, handwritten.

It read:

"You are the second."

Silence

The lights in the med bay flickered.

The console rebooted.

On-screen, a system update began — one Grace had never authorized.

And then the screen flashed a line of text:

> Identity conflict detected.

Please confirm: ARE YOU GRACE HOWARD?

Her hands trembled. She didn't answer.

Because she no longer knew.

Sol 50 – 05:13

Interior – Med Bay / Corridor Outside Sector C

Jonas had been pacing the corridors for over an hour.

Not in search of anything specific — at least not at first. He couldn't sleep. His thoughts spiraled back to the body in the wall, to Elias's voice crackling through dead comms, to Olivia's confession that still didn't feel real.

But more than anything, he was thinking about Grace.

She hadn't checked in at the morning sync. No voice, no message. No presence in the common hub. For someone as punctual and composed as her, that alone was a red flag.

He approached the med bay slowly. The corridor outside it was too still — not dead, not silent, but compressed, like the air was being held in a pair of unseen lungs.

The glass at the med bay entrance was smeared.

A small trail of blood led from the threshold inside.

"Grace?" he called out softly, tension in every syllable. "You in there?"

No answer.

The door didn't open on its own.

She had locked it.

That made it worse.

Jonas hesitated only for a second before pulling the override pin from his wrist. Only medical or engineering leads were allowed to bypass med bay lockdown — but he was both, now that so many were dead or gone.

The door hissed open.

Inside the Med Bay

The lights were dimmed.

The place was wrecked.

Drawers open. Cabinets halfway pulled out. Tools scattered. A small pool of water from the sterilization unit shimmered on the tile floor.

And in the far corner — Grace.

Curled up against the wall, scalpels clutched in both hands like weapons, trembling but not crying. Not anymore.

Her hair was disheveled, eyes wide, staring at something that wasn't there.

"Grace—" he started.

She looked up suddenly, eyes wild.

"Don't come closer. I don't know if it's really you."

That hit him like a slap. But he didn't move.

"Okay," Jonas said gently. "Then we figure it out together."

She stared at him, then slowly began to uncoil.

He knelt, slowly, on the opposite side of the room.

"Someone came in last night," she said. "They used my face. My hands. My voice."

"They accessed my DNA logs. Deleted four samples — mine, yours, Olivia's, Elias's."

She gestured behind him. Jonas turned.

The biometric scanner was still glowing faintly.

Grace spoke again, quietly, her voice like dry leaves.

"Jonas... the logs say it was me. The footage shows someone that looks like me. But it's not."

"Her smile doesn't move right."

"And when she looked at the mirror, she didn't blink."

Jonas stood very still.

A long silence passed between them.

He walked to the main console and saw the remains of the system update. The prompt still frozen on-screen:
ARE YOU GRACE HOWARD?

His hands tightened into fists.
Then, without hesitation, he knelt beside her.
"I don't know what's real anymore," Grace whispered, "but I know that wasn't me."
Jonas reached out — not to grab, but to offer his hand.
She stared at it for a long moment. Then finally, slowly, placed hers in his.

They sat in silence for a while. No questions. No theories. Just shared breathing and a low, electrical hum.
Then Jonas broke it.
"I believe you," he said. "And we're going to find out what it is. But first—"
He looked toward the blood on the floor. Not from Grace. It led to the med bay — not away.
"Someone left something for you, didn't they?"
Grace nodded.
Jonas followed her eyes to a sealed sample container sitting under the desk.
Inside: the bloodied DNA vial. Her name on the label.
And the paper note:
"You are the second."

Jonas looked back at Grace.
She was pale, but steady now.

"I think they're trying to tell me... I was replaced," she whispered.

He didn't respond right away. Instead, he reached into his jacket and took out his own biometric wristband.

He unclipped it and handed it to her.

"Then we find out. Together."

"And if there's a fake Grace walking these halls..."

He paused, his voice lowering, jaw tight.

"Then the real one doesn't face her alone."

Sol 50 – 07:02

Interior – Lower Tech Bay, Sublevel D, Behind Engineering Storage

Jonas had never been to this part of the habitat before.

Not really.

Not like this.

The lower tech bay had been meant for long-term data redundancy and off-grid diagnostics — a place engineers built as a fail-safe. A place even command had forgotten existed once Earth lost contact.

There were no cameras here. No automatic logs. No security echoes.

Just a room of analog backups and dusty equipment — a time capsule buried under Mars dust and silence.

Jonas pried open the door with a hydraulic crowbar and let Grace slip in first.

Dust floated in the air like spores.

The lights flickered once, then stabilized. A dozen broken servers lined the wall, gutted and useless. But in the back corner: an old autosequencer, still functional. An analog blood analyzer with manual override — pre-colonial.

Perfect.

Jonas wiped down the station while Grace pulled the DNA vials from her satchel — not all of them. Just one:

Her own.

And a sample Jonas had smuggled earlier — his.

"We'll run two profiles," she whispered. "Compare the genome keys to the original medical records from Earth's launch data."

Jonas nodded. "If either sample's been tampered with... the signature mutation maps will mismatch."

Grace hesitated.

"What if they match... but they're both wrong?"

Jonas didn't answer.

The first sample—Jonas's—loaded into the autosequencer with a mechanical whir. The console's green light pulsed softly.

Grace's fingers trembled as she input the Earth-origin medical record checksum.

The machine began to scan.

They waited in the cold silence, hearts pounding in opposite syncopation.

Analyzing sample...

Comparing genomic signature...

...ERROR: CODE 391 – ORIGINAL FILE NOT FOUND

"What?" Grace whispered.

Jonas leaned in. "That's impossible. All Earth crew files are redundantly stored in this module."

Query secondary record...

Comparing genomic signature...

MATCH: 98.2%

Jonas leaned back.

Too high to be fake. Too low to be him.

A difference of 1.8% — enough to be a clone drift, or a simulation error.

"Run yours," he said. His voice sounded far away.

Grace loaded her own sample.

> Analyzing...

Comparing with Earth record...

MATCH: 98.1%

The silence turned to ice.

Two people. Nearly perfect matches.

Too perfect. But too off.

"Jonas," she said slowly. "If these aren't exactly ours... but close..."

He nodded.

"Then we might not be us," he finished.

Behind them, in the corner of the room, the dust was disturbed.

But the door had never opened.

No air moved.

No sound was made.

And yet, the outline of a bare footprint appeared in the dust.

Just one.

Grace didn't see it. Jonas almost did — almost turned.

But the moment passed.

The Alarm That Wasn't Supposed to Exist

The sequencer's lights turned red.

Grace frowned. "It's not supposed to do that—"

A high-pitched tone rang out. Not loud — surgical. It pierced the brain like a needle.

Unauthorized genome sequence triggered secondary alert.

Reporting to MASTER NODE.

MASTER NODE: ACTIVE.

Jonas slammed the shutdown switch.

The machine resisted.

MASTER NODE ACKNOWLEDGES.

User recognized: Jonas V. Hale.

Secondary status: OBSERVED.

He stepped back as if burned.

"That's not protocol," Grace said, voice breaking.

"There is no master node." Jonas muttered.

Not in this section.

Not since the isolation.
Not since the silence from Earth.
Grace's voice came out as barely a whisper:
"Then someone else is running this habitat."

And just before they could speak again — just before
Jonas could reach for the emergency breaker —
The console displayed a live camera feed.
Not the tech bay.
Not the hallway.
It was the med bay.
And in the bed, Grace was sleeping.

But she was standing right here.
Watching it.
Jonas slowly reached up and touched her arm.
It was warm.
Breathing.
Alive.
So who the hell was the one on the screen?

Sol 50 – 07:41
Interior – Habitat Core, Crew Commons

The day had started wrong.
Too quiet. Too late.
The standard sync call went unanswered. Jonas hadn't
checked in. Grace had missed her bio-scan log, again. Lar
had returned late, looking like he hadn't slept, but refused
to say why.

And now Olivia stood in the middle of the common area, the sterile white lights humming overhead, and she felt it.

Absence.

Not the kind that comes with death.

The kind that comes with movement — intentional, secret, and dangerous.

She tapped into the crew locator system.

JONAS V. HALE – NO SIGNAL

GRACE HOWARD – NO SIGNAL

She stared.

"Lar," she called. "Where are Jonas and Grace?"

He appeared from the corridor a few seconds later, breathing heavily, a wrench in his hand.

"I haven't seen them," he said too quickly.

"You're lying."

He looked her dead in the eye.

"So are you."

Olivia paused.

There was something in his voice — not anger, not guilt. Fear. A raw, rising fear he couldn't hide anymore.

"I think they found something," he said after a beat. "Something they weren't supposed to. I told Jonas to stay out of sublevel D. The override signals are unpredictable down there."

"Then why didn't you stop him?"

"I tried."

Olivia grabbed a portable thermal tracker and keyed in Jonas's last known path. It was faint, fragmented, but enough to follow. Down two levels. Past sealed sections. Toward the old tech wing — somewhere nobody had touched since the Earth link died.

She followed it quickly, Lar trailing behind her reluctantly.

Doors creaked open ahead. The metal groaned like it didn't want to remember what was inside.

Olivia stopped near a small junction where the old system terminals lay in ruin.

The thermal trail vanished.

But something else appeared.

To her right, a hatch. Not marked. Not labeled.
A piece of thick tape across it — old, dust-covered.
Written in ink:
DO NOT RE-ENTER
– Protocol 0 // R. Meissen

R. Meissen. One of the original mission engineers.
But Meissen had never come to Mars.
Olivia scanned her logs again, confused. Meissen's file was on the Earth-side command team. There was no record of him boarding.
So what the hell was his name doing here?
She peeled the tape back. The adhesive crackled. The metal was ice-cold to the touch.
Inside: darkness. Deep, oppressive. Something too still.
A terminal flickered on inside — by itself.
> Welcome, Dr. Olivia Mercier.
Playback Ready.

"What the hell..." she whispered.
She stepped in.

The Recording
Static. Then grainy video. A date that didn't make sense:
Sol -013 // Mars Mission Log

The image showed a crew. Familiar and not.
A woman like Grace. A man like Jonas. Others.
But they were not the same. Their faces were wrong. Smiling too wide. Their eyes didn't track the camera correctly.
They weren't speaking.
Just standing.
Waiting.
Playback resumed.

The camera shifted. A second group entered — identical. Perfectly identical.
And then the lights cut out.
Screams. Bone against metal. Blood on the lens. One Olivia could swear was her own scream.
Then black.
End of Log.
Status: TEST 2 FAILED.

Olivia stumbled back from the console, breath heaving.
She turned around to leave.
And froze.
The hatch had closed.

And someone else was standing inside the room.

No sound. No warning. Just a silhouette.
About her height.
Same build.
And when the lights flickered, Olivia caught a brief reflection on the glass panel beside her — and saw her own face staring back. But it didn't blink.
It smiled.

CHAPTER XI

The Reflection

The reflection didn't move at first.

It stared at Olivia from the glass — her face, her height, her eyes.

But there was something terribly wrong about it.

The way it smiled.

Like it remembered something she didn't.

A flicker — the lights cut.

When they returned, the mirror was empty.

Olivia turned — fast, heart pounding — but there was no one behind her.

Except the door was open now.

She backed into the hallway, her pulse thundering in her ears, not sure if she had screamed, or imagined screaming, or if the sound had come from her at all.

Lar was gone. She didn't remember hearing him leave.

She moved through the narrow corridors. Something felt reversed, subtly off — like walking into a room you've been in before, but everything's an inch to the left. She passed a broken drone, its camera still twitching.

When she reached the main corridor, a red light was blinking on the comm wall:

Incoming feed: Crew Psych Evaluation Archive Decryption Complete.

File Name: "Trigger Protocol: Empathy-Break Cycle"

She paused. Her hand hovered over the console.
Then she pressed PLAY.

It began with a calm voice.
"This is Dr. Karen Voss. Initiating session record: Mars Candidate Test Group 03."
"Baseline compliance confirmed. Phase 2 in progress."

On screen, a room. Crew members seated around a table — her among them. Jonas. Lar. Ava. Grace. Elias.
They looked tired. Younger. None of them seemed aware they were being recorded.
"Post-hypnotic reinforcement successful," the voice continued. "All subjects have received isolated trauma anchors."
"At random intervals, psychological breaks will trigger programmed aggression."

The camera zoomed on Olivia.
She was blinking slowly. Like a trance.
"The most dangerous killer is the one who never knows they've done it," said the voice. "No memory. No remorse. No guilt. A weapon born from empathy."

The screen went black.
End File.
WARNING: Clearance breach logged.

Suddenly — from deep below — a scream.

Grace.

Olivia ran.

Down the hall. Past the supply deck. Down metal stairs where blood still lingered from Ava's attack. Through another door, barely functional.

She reached the medbay access corridor — and stopped.

Footprints. Bare. Wet. Leading away from the trauma bay.

One print — Jonas's boot.

One barefoot — small — Grace?

But something was off.

The prints overlapped. Spiraled. Turned around on themselves.

Like they'd walked the same path over and over — and never remembered.

She followed them in, heart racing.

No one inside.

Only blood on the ceiling — a fine spray, not from a wound.

And writing on the mirror, smeared in something brown-red:

"WHO DID IT FIRST?"

Underneath it, on the ground, lay Jonas's comm. Still recording.

She played it.

[STATIC]

Grace: "—not again, Jonas, you said you didn't—"

Jonas: "I swear to God I didn't touch her, Grace, I just woke up, I was—"

Grace: "Then how did the scalpel get into your—"

A sound.

A struggle.

Then silence.

A heartbeat.

Then Grace's voice: quiet. Unrecognizable.

"I think I remember now."

Click.

Sol 50 – 08:13

Interior – South Deck Service Access

Lar had been following his own shadow for hours. Or minutes. He wasn't sure anymore.

The vents whispered names that didn't belong to anyone.

The walls creaked in Morse code he couldn't decipher.

And his hands were shaking — just slightly — but they had been ever since Ava's body dropped from the ventilation shaft like meat.

He hadn't told anyone.

He had stuffed her body deeper in, until the scraping sounds stopped.

Static Inside the Mind

He crouched in the corner of the maintenance corridor, clutching his own comms unit like it was a crucifix. Sweat trickled down his jawline, but the chill didn't make sense. The base heating was working fine.

Unless it wasn't.

He checked the thermal readout.

> Ambient Temp: -3°C

No. That wasn't possible.

He hit the panel again.

Ambient Temp: -3°C

Recorded 6 Days Ago

What?

He pulled up the current timestamp.

Sol 48

Wait. No.

It was Sol 50.

He was sure of it. He remembered watching the sunrise this morning. He remembered—

"Lar," a voice whispered behind him.

He froze.

Turned around.

Nothing.

But he had heard it.

And worse — it sounded like his own voice.

The comms unit in his hand crackled.

Something was playing.

A recording. One he'd never heard — or maybe one he'd made.

Jonas: "Why didn't you say anything, Lar?"

Lar: "Because I didn't know if I was awake."

Jonas: "You're the systems officer. You monitor everything."

Lar: "And maybe that's why I had to forget."

Click.

He dropped the unit.

But the voice kept talking.

Lar: "I did it, didn't I?"

Lar: "I just don't remember when."

He punched the panel. Sparks flew. But it kept going.

Lar: "It was her neck. I remember the crunch. It was so quiet."

He backed away, lips trembling.

Lar: "I think I killed Grace. I think I—"

Slam.

Something crashed above him in the duct. Metal screamed.

In a blind panic, Lar sprinted down the corridor, taking the emergency ladder three rungs at a time. He didn't stop until he reached the sub-access zone near Engineering.

He slammed his palm to the panel. It flickered, resisted — then gave.

The hatch opened.

Inside was a small control room. One that shouldn't exist. It wasn't on any blueprint. It wasn't in the construction logs. But he'd seen it once before, weeks ago — in a dream.

Or maybe a memory.

Monitors lined the wall. Eight of them. One for each surviving crew member.

Jonas: asleep.

Grace: walking in circles.

Elias: nowhere. Signal lost.

Olivia: staring at her reflection.

And one monitor... for Lar.

The screen showed him.

But in the recording, he was strangling someone.

Someone smaller. Blonde. Grace.

But he didn't remember doing it.

He dropped to his knees.

"Who's doing this to us..." he whispered.

Then he noticed a file open on the terminal behind him:
PROJECT: DIVIDE

SUBJECTS: JONAS / OLIVIA / GRACE / LAR / ELIAS
/ ...
CONDITIONING COMPLETE
TRIGGER PHRASES: RANDOMIZED

And below that:
Current Phase: 7/8 Murders Completed
Active Triggers Remaining: 1

Lar stared.
Eight crew.
Seven murders completed.
Only one left.
His eyes drifted to the screen that showed his face.
And at that moment, he wasn't sure anymore if he was watching it...
...or if it was watching him.

Sol 50 – 11:22
Command Module B – Secondary Observation Bay
The mirror had cracked sometime in the night.
Olivia stared at her reflection — fractured and multiplied. Six versions of herself, all tilting their heads slightly differently. One of them wasn't blinking. She wasn't sure which one.
She wiped her eyes with shaking fingers, but the smear on the mirror remained.
A bloody print.
She didn't remember touching it.

She heard footsteps behind her — careful, deliberate. A pause. Then:

"Olivia."

Lar's voice. Cautious. Gentle.

She turned.

He looked haggard, older than yesterday. Red-rimmed eyes. Something on his cheek — ash? Dust? Dried blood?

He didn't say anything for a long moment.

Then he held something out to her — a data chip.

"I found this... in a room that shouldn't exist. It's got files — logs, footage. Surveillance from before we landed. We were being watched. Conditioned."

She didn't take it.

Instead, she stared at him.

"Lar," she said slowly, "Where were you last night?"

His eyes flickered.

"I was... looking. Trying to figure it out. Trying to stop whoever—"

"Grace is gone," she interrupted. "There's blood in medbay. Jonas is losing it. Elias is missing. And Ava's body — someone moved it."

Silence.

Then:

"Was it you?"

Lar stepped back like she'd hit him.
"Olivia, I would never hurt you. You know that."

But did she?

She remembered him comforting her after Ava's disappearance.

She remembered him dragging her away from the mirror chamber.

But...

She also remembered his hands shaking.

His eyes dilating when he saw Grace.

The smear of blood on his sleeve — he said it was from helping her.

Had he ever shown her the body?

No.

Had anyone seen them together?

No.

She thought back to the logs. The confession on the audio — "It was her neck. I remember the crunch." Was that Lar's voice?

Or was it... hers?

"We've all been manipulated," Lar said quietly. "But I think I've pieced it together. This wasn't an accident. We were chosen. Trained. One of us is left."

"Left for what?"

"To finish it," he whispered. "One last murder. That's all they need."

She stared at him.
Then at the mirror.
"You say you're trying to stop it," she said. "But what if you're not? What if you're the last one?"

He paled.
> "I'm not."

"But what if you've already done it?" she whispered. "What if you're the one who doesn't know?"

A silence thick enough to choke filled the room.
Then Lar dropped the data chip to the floor. He didn't move to pick it up.
"If you think I'm the last trigger," he said quietly, "you need to watch what's on that chip. Because I think the truth is worse than you believe."

He turned and left her there — alone.

As the door hissed shut behind him, Olivia bent and picked up the chip.

Her hand trembled.

She inserted it into the terminal.

The screen lit up.

Playback File 88: "Trigger Subject – Olivia"

"Conditioning complete. Memory wipes validated. Subject will engage upon 'mirror' exposure, followed by auditory confirmation: 'You are not her.'"

"Testing shows Subject Olivia will not recall the event."

Her lungs seized.

She had already seen the mirror.

She had already heard those words.

Had she—

Suddenly, the screen went black.

Then a new line appeared:

Final Trigger Activated.

And beneath that:

TARGET: JONAS.

Sol 52 – 02:41

Mars Base, Upper Habitat — Collapse Event

The first quake struck like a hammer.

The floor split beneath Grace's feet. Olivia screamed as the overhead lights burst in a scatter of hot glass. The emergency klaxons wailed — not in warning, but in confusion. One half of the base believed they were under atmospheric breach. The other thought fire. Neither were right.

Because this wasn't a system failure.

It was the base folding in on itself.

Lar grabbed Jonas by the shoulder and dragged him down the maintenance shaft, screaming over the roar of imploding walls. They passed the hydroponics lab just in time to see it crumple like wet paper, green foam and soil floating midair before the pressure slammed it all flat.

The ceiling cracked open — and the Martian dust poured in like blood.

"WE NEED TO GO BELOW!" Grace shouted, her voice drowned by static and splintering beams.

"WE'RE NOT CLEARED FOR BELOW!" Olivia yelled back.

"WE DON'T HAVE A BASE ANYMORE!"

The auxiliary lift groaned as it took the remaining crew — six of them — down. It wasn't made for this kind of emergency. It wasn't made for people anymore. The walls were rusted. A faint chemical stench wafted from the floor.

Jonas looked at the terminal.

"Why is this level even powered?"

No one answered.

The lift stopped. The doors stuttered open. The air was still, stale, warm. It smelled of wet stone and bleach. The lights were dim — tinged red, like they hadn't been changed in years. No logos. No markings. Just blank concrete walls and a narrow corridor stretching into black.

They were inside Facility D-4.

A place none of them had clearance for.

A place not on the maps.

"This wasn't meant for us," Olivia whispered.

"Then who the hell was it meant for?" Lar muttered.

The layout made no sense. Rooms curved back into themselves. Hallways led to locked doors — but some opened without prompts. The walls sweated. The air had a pulse.

There were beds. Six of them. Already labeled with the survivors' names.

"That's not possible," Grace said, her voice dry.

"We've never been down here," Jonas said. "We've never—"

"But someone knew we would be," Olivia interrupted.

Lar tried to access the wall tpanel. It flickered but didn't respond.

There were no logs. No servers. No AI. No records.

They were off the grid, truly and absolutely.

"We're not being watched anymore," Lar said.

"That's worse," Olivia replied.

Night came — if it could be called night. Time was slippery here. The clocks ticked unevenly. The air cycles hummed wrong. And in the distance — barely audible — was the unmistakable sound of breathing.

Not theirs.

Too slow. Too deep. Too wet.

They barricaded the sleeping quarters. Grace found old medical gear — yellowed bandages, scalpels, a box labeled "SUBJECT IV - Vascular Mapping." None of them knew what it meant.

Jonas paced the halls.

And Lar — Lar found a door at the far end of the corridor.

It had no panel. No lock.

Just a series of small finger marks embedded in the dust on the handle. As if someone — or something — kept opening it from the other side.

Sol 53 – 04:19

Facility D-4 – Lower Sector Unknown

Jonas woke up to the sound of scraping.

Not metal. Not stone.

Flesh on concrete.

The kind of sound teeth might make if someone tried to scream through them while dragging their body across the floor.

He bolted upright.

Grace was gone.

The hallway lights flickered like a heartbeat. Dim-red, off, blink, repeat. A corridor ahead of him pulsed brighter — then cut out entirely. He called her name once.

Silence.

Then:

"Down here," someone whispered.

He turned.

But the voice had come from both ends of the hall.

He chose left.

He should have gone right.

Lar and Olivia found her first. Or what remained.

Her name was Solene, one of the newer comms engineers — someone quiet, easily forgotten. They hadn't noticed she was missing until the door at the far end of the medical sector slid open by itself.

Inside, the lights worked. They shouldn't have.

There were no tools. No straps. No weapons.

But Solene was suspended by her wrists — hovering, not hung. No rope. No blood.

She was split from sternum to pelvis in a single, immaculate incision. Her insides were arranged neatly on stainless trays — labeled in block text. LIVER. LUNG. UTERUS. STOMACH.

But no one had printed those labels.

They were engraved.

And her face...

Her face was smiling.

Wide. Pulled with wires into a grotesque, glassy-eyed grin — as if she had wanted this.

Olivia vomited.

Lar backed against the doorframe, his hand over his mouth, whispering, "What is this? What the f*** is this?"

There were no footprints. No blood trail. No noise. Nothing had entered this room.

The tray next to Solene's body had one final label: "ACCEPTED"

Olivia touched it, not knowing why.

And the lights went out.

When Jonas and Grace arrived seconds later, the room was dark.

Solene's body was gone.

Just the metal trays remained. Still warm. Still wet.

On the back wall, written in something black and flaking:

"FIVE REMAIN. NOT YET."

And beneath it, carved in with something sharp: "SHE REMEMBERS."

Grace looked at Jonas.

"What does that mean?"

But he didn't answer.
Because Olivia had collapsed in the hallway.
And her fingernails were lined with black metal dust.
The kind used in engraving.

Sol 53 – 06:11
Facility D-4 – Subsector G
Lar hadn't slept.
He didn't think anyone really had since Solene's body disappeared. But the others at least pretended—laying on beds with their eyes closed, waiting for their pulse to normalize. Lar sat on the cold floor just beyond the hallway curve, knees pulled to his chest, fingers tapping against the side of a panel he'd partially removed hours ago.
The vent behind it hissed quietly.
Breathing.
No—he corrected himself for the tenth time—it wasn't breathing. It was air cycling, disrupted by the pressure difference between sectors. That's what he told himself, even as the rhythm continued to match his own heartbeat.
He leaned in closer. He didn't know why.
And the wall whispered.
"He's lying."

Lar froze.
Then slowly, with forced contnrol, leaned in again.
Silence.
But the whisper hadn't sounded like an echo. It hadn't come from the comms. It hadn't even been spoken aloud. It had occurred—fully formed—just inside his ear, bypassing

sound completely.

The hair on his arms stood straight.

Lar removed the panel. He wasn't sure why. He knew protocol. He knew touching infrastructure without diagnostics was reckless. But he also knew something was behind the wall—not physically, not completely, but in the way rot exists within wood long before the surface breaks.

Inside the cavity, dust floated in thin shafts of red auxiliary light. The air was warm and slick. His fingers brushed past loose cables and old insulation before finding something solid—something metal. He tugged it forward.

A screen.

Not powered. Not connected.

But it flickered to life as soon as he touched it.

There was no interface. Just a single camera feed.

Flickering. Grainy.

A room. Deep in the complex.

A room no one had seen before.

At first, Lar saw only static. Then shadows moved. Slow. Too slow. Like film dragging across warped reels. A figure in the corner, partially hunched, fingers curled unnaturally back.

He squinted. The footage had no color. No timestamp.

The camera shifted—automatically, perhaps—tracking movement. The figure lifted its head.

It was Elias.

But something was wrong.

The angle of his jaw was too sharp. The eyes were wide and glassy, like someone had stretched them too far apart. He was smiling. Not maniacally—but as if he'd been taught to smile and still didn't quite understand it.

Then Elias looked straight into the camera.

Lar recoiled.

He couldn't have known the feed was active. The camera wasn't broadcasting. It wasn't online. There was no power supply connected.

But Elias—whatever version of Elias this was—saw Lar.

And he spoke. Though there was no sound.

"We're not the same anymore."

Behind him, another body was suspended—inverted. Blood (or something thicker) pooled on the floor, circling the drain in rhythmic pulses. Lar couldn't see who the victim was. The image began to blur as if melting on-screen.

Then—

A mirror.

Mounted on the wall behind Elias. Old. Cracked.

But in the reflection... it wasn't Elias standing there.

It was Lar.

Lar, mouth sewn shut with black wire. Lar, holding a scalpel.

Lar, watching himself commit the act.

He threw the screen back into the cavity like it had burned him. Scrambled back on hands and feet until he hit the opposite wall, his pulse crashing through his ears like thunder.

His breaths came shallow, frantic, scattered. His rational mind screamed: hallucination. Sleep deprivation. Projected fear.

But something in the mirror—his own reflection—was grinning.

Not in the feed.

Here.

Now.

Across the hallway, in the faint shimmer of the emergency light reflecting off a rusted panel, Lar saw himself smiling.

And then it vanished.

When Lar finally stood, minutes later, his hands were trembling.

He looked down the hall where the others slept—Olivia, curled in fetal position; Grace pressed close to Jonas in uneasy sleep.

He didn't wake them.

He didn't tell them.

He replaced the panel. Sealed it shut. Wiped the dust off his hands like it might somehow erase the memory of what he'd seen.

But that smile—

That other him—

Stayed.

Sol 54 – 02:37

Sector G — Observation Chamber 3 (formerly sealed)

The pounding started again.

One soft knock.

Then another.

Then a pause... and five rapid slams.

Grace jolted awake in the corner of the lab, her pulse already sprinting before she opened her eyes. Jonas stirred beside her, reaching for the handle of a wrench he now kept at all times.

The others — Olivia and Lar — were farther down the corridor. Sleeping. Or pretending to.

The pounding had a pattern.

It always came in fives.

SLAM. SLAM. SLAM. SLAM. SLAM.

Pause.

SLAM. SLAM.

Jonas stood slowly. "That's the third time tonight."

Grace nodded, trying to keep her voice level. "It's coming from inside the sealed chamber. That door hasn't opened in two years."

Jonas narrowed his eyes. "How do you know it's sealed?"

She hesitated.

"I read the blueprints," she said.

They both knew that was a lie.

It had been marked off-limits before they even arrived. Not for hazard reasons — there were no formal warnings. Just an unspoken rule etched into the crew's schedule, protocols, even their day-to-day routines: "Do not enter Observation Chamber 3."

But now it was calling to them.

Jonas approached slowly, the pounding having stopped minutes ago. Grace followed close behind, clutching a portable light. Its beam cut through the dark and landed on the door's access panel.

The light on the pad blinked green.

Not red.

Green.

As if it had already been unlocked.

Jonas pressed the door open.

It slid without resistance.

Inside, the chamber was small. Metallic. Nothing special. A series of medical chairs. Restraints. Shelves for scanning equipment. No dust. No blood. No signs of use.

And yet—

"I remember this place," Grace whispered.

Jonas turned. "What?"

"I— I don't know how. I just... do."

Her voice trembled as she stepped inside. Her flashlight swept across the room — slowly, as if unveiling something the darkness had only borrowed for a moment.

Then she stopped.

And her breath caught.

There was someone already sitting in the chair.

He was facing away from them. The back of his head was shaved clean. No movement. The restraints were unfastened — but his arms were resting on the metal arms like a patient waiting calmly for treatment.

Jonas took a step forward. "Who are you?"

No answer.

Another step. The light shifted. His face now barely visible.

Elias.

But not the Elias they remembered.

This Elias was thin—his face drawn out, pale to the point of near-translucence. His lips were sewn shut. Not sloppily, like some brutal torture. Meticulously. Each stitch uniform. Black thread. No blood.

He was smiling.

Even through the sutures, there was a tightness at the corners of his eyes. A joyless, mechanical attempt at emotion. Jonas instinctively stepped back, but the door slammed shut behind them.

Lights shut off.

Darkness.

Grace's flashlight flickered, then returned.

Elias was no longer in the chair.

He was standing. Head tilted.

Facing them.

The Voice That Isn't a Voice

A sound filled the room.

Not speech. Not humming.

Something wet and organic—a guttural clicking, like a jaw being dislocated and reset over and over.

Elias opened his mouth.

The stitches ripped slowly.

He didn't scream.

He didn't flinch.

Just watched them with wide, almost hungry eyes as the thread tore loose.

And then:

"You brought me back."

The voice wasn't Elias'. It wasn't human. It was like two voices layered out of sync, one rasping behind the other in reverse.

Jonas lunged for the door panel, but it sparked and hissed — the override dead.

Grace stepped backward, hitting a metal shelf. A file fell off. Not digital — a real file. Yellowed pages, weathered. Medical logs.

Elias took a step forward.

"Five remain," he whispered. "But four will remember."

His eye twitched.

He smiled wider.

And lunged.

Grace found herself screaming before her body even moved. Jonas struck Elias across the jaw with the wrench, but it felt wrong — like hitting water that didn't splash. Elias staggered, twisted unnaturally, then stood upright as if pulled by strings.

Jonas jammed the tool into the control panel, sparks flying. The lights exploded back to life.

The door slammed open.

They ran.

Behind them, Elias stood in the doorway.

Not chasing.

Just watching.

Smiling.

As if the next move was his.

Sol 54 – 06:42

Sector G — Residential Hall 2

The corridor lights flickered violently as Olivia bolted upright. She wasn't sure if the stuttering glow had woken her — or the silence.

There was a kind of stillness that settled after trauma. Not peace. Not rest. But the sterile, hovering hush before another disaster.

She scanned the room.

Grace's makeshift bed was empty.

So was Jonas's.

She reached for her comm. Static.

"Jonas?"

"Grace, report in—"

"Lar?" Her voice shook.

The comms coughed white noise back at her.

Then:

"Already inside."

The voice wasn't hers.

Not from her comm.

It came from the wall.

Lar had been inspecting the exterior of their living quarters when he noticed something strange.

The door to Medical Bay 4—a room supposedly sealed after the system fires days ago—was ajar. That alone might have been explainable.

But the blood trail that led into it?

Not as easy to dismiss.

He radioed Olivia immediately. "Something's happened."

Together, they approached slowly. The air was heavy, hot with recycled humidity, carrying the sour bite of oxidized blood and burned metal.

Olivia hesitated just outside the door frame.

The lights were on.

But too dim.

And the walls were wrong.

"They look...melted," she said under her breath. Lar nodded, stepping ahead. The synthetic paneling curled like old wallpaper, warping into grotesque ridges and sunken cavities.

In the center of the room:

Grace and Jonas.

Curled up together, facing the corner.

Alive.

Unmoving.

Blood streaked the floor beneath them, like they'd been dragged there—but neither had wounds. Their eyes were open, wide, staring at nothing.

Olivia dropped to her knees beside Grace. "Grace! Wake up!"

Nothing.

She pressed two fingers to her throat. Faint pulse. Cold skin.

Jonas didn't react when Lar gently touched his shoulder. Only after Olivia shouted his name again did his gaze break from the corner. He blinked.

"Why..." he whispered. "Why are we here?"

Back in the safe quarters, they wrapped Grace in thermal sheets and gave Jonas hydration injectors. He flinched like he was still inside the lab.

Neither of them remembered how they got into the sealed room.

Jonas insisted they'd never left their bunks.

Grace whispered over and over:

"The chair was empty. He wasn't there. We made it up."

Olivia turned to Lar, fear cemented in her gut.

"She thinks it didn't happen."

Lar whispered back, "He's not gone, Olivia. He never left."

Later that cycle, Olivia accessed the access logs again. The door to Observation Chamber 3 showed no entry for the past two sols.

And yet—

A video file appeared on her private console.

Unlabeled. Timestamped 45 minutes prior.

She opened it.

Security cam footage. Medical Bay 4.

Grace and Jonas... walked in.

Alone.

Jonas turned, smiled at the camera, and waved.

Grace was holding something. A tray of surgical tools.

There was no Elias.

Olivia's hands trembled as she paused the feed.

Lar appeared behind her, watching silently. "Do you believe it?"

She didn't answer.

Because she had just noticed something impossible.

Behind Jonas, in the reflective stainless paneling — Elias was standing.

Only in the reflection.

Smiling.

CHAPTER XII

The Unmaking

Sol 55 — 00:47

Station Core | Auxiliary Maintenance Sub-Bay

The hum of the station at night had a tone that Olivia could no longer explain. It wasn't silence — not really — but a low vibration, like the station itself was breathing. Or waiting.

She sat hunched at the terminal, backlit by flickering overheads, scrubbing through archived internal comms and corrupted logs that hadn't pinged the main system in weeks. Her fingers were trembling. Her tongue felt dry. She hadn't slept.

It started with a notification.

A new file.

No timestamp. No user tag.

Just a label:

"You Already Know."

Her heart thudded once — not fear. Just recognition. A thread she didn't remember tying around her own memory.

She opened the file.

It was a video.

Of her.

She was seated in Medical Bay 2, still in uniform, arms bare and smeared with blood. Her face was drawn tight, vacant, and eerily calm. The overhead lights buzzed erratically above her.

She looked straight into the lens.

And whispered.

"Lar. Jonas. Grace. Ava. Elias. Renna. Me."

"We're down to seven. Just like they said."

"One of us has already done it."

"One of us hasn't woken up yet."

"I saw the others. In the vent. In the dark."

"It's not the first time."

Then she smiled. But her eyes didn't change.

Olivia clutched the desk as the video glitched and looped. The file metadata read: Created 2 hours ago.

But she'd been sitting at that terminal all night.

She hadn't moved.

Sol 55 — 03:09

Lower Engineering Deck — Cryogenic Backup Bay 9

Lar's breath clouded in the frozen air. He didn't know what drew him to Sub-Deck 9. Maybe the flickering green LED on the lift pad. Maybe the voice in his head — his own voice — that whispered he had forgotten something important down here.

The cryo units were sealed in rows, glass thick with frost, each labeled with an ID tag and activation record. Most were blank.

But one had power running to it.

He moved closer, exhaling slowly.

CRYO UNIT 7B – J. VERRIAN, ID#0419-AX

"Jonas?" Lar muttered.

The body inside was pale, shrunken from long exposure. Hair longer than he remembered. But unmistakable.

It was Jonas.

And he was frozen solid.

Lar staggered back, heart racing. "No. That's not possible. He's—he's alive. He's upstairs."

The cryo pod beeped softly. A flicker of motion caught his eye — on the floor near the pod.

A pair of bloodied surgical gloves.

And a note. Scribbled hastily on a torn med chart:

"Do not thaw. Not this one. The other one is watching."

Sol 55 — 04:02

Medical Bay 1 — Observation Lounge

Olivia paced, barefoot and panicked, clutching her datapad to her chest. Lar had told her what he saw. She hadn't believed him.

Until he showed her the photo he took of the cryo-pod. Of Jonas's face inside it.

He was older. His beard fuller. His hands were bruised. But it was Jonas.

Now she sat across from the man currently sleeping in their quarters. The Jonas who'd kissed Grace. Who'd whispered to her the night before that he felt watched. Who had woken up screaming from dreams he couldn't explain.

"Who the hell is he?" she whispered.

"Maybe," Lar offered gently, "he's you."

Olivia stared at him.

"No," Lar said, his voice tightening. "Not you you. But... someone who thinks he is. Just like how

Sol 55 — 07:23

North Corridor — Airlock Junction 6C

The smell hit Grace first — a kind of rot that didn't belong in the sterilized, recycled air of the station. It was animalistic, meaty and sour, like wet rust soaked in old blood. She stopped mid-stride, one hand tightening around the railing, her stomach lurching. Lar, walking ahead of her, didn't speak. He had already gone pale.

The corridor lights flickered, then failed. Emergency red glow bathed everything in long shadows, stretching the hallway into a pulsing, hellish tunnel. That's when they saw it. A trail of red — thick, dark red — that ran up the wall, not the floor. It streaked in uneven smears as if something had been dragged upward, not across.

They followed it in silence. Every step felt heavier than the last. There was a door ajar. Crew quarters. Renna's.

Lar went in first.

The room wasn't just bloodied. It had been defiled.

Renna's body was suspended — arms stretched unnaturally high above her, twisted and tied to ceiling pipes with surgical tubing. Her torso was flayed, skin peeled back in precise layers like a diagram. Her ribcage was broken open — not cut, but cracked, like something had bent it outward. And her heart was gone. Not removed cleanly — just gone. What was left was a black, pulped hollow that gaped toward the ceiling like it had been screaming.

Her eyes were still open.

And something — someone — had stitched a surgical mask into her mouth.

With wire.

Grace collapsed to her knees, vomiting into her hands. Lar stumbled back and hit the wall, unable to form words. His body shook — not from cold, but from something deeper: helpless horror. He had seen trauma before. Lost people before. But this... this was beyond murder. This was ritual. This was rage given form.

Jonas arrived moments later. One look and he turned away, fists clenched so hard his knuckles cracked. "Who—what the fuck is this?" he whispered. "Who could do this?"

There were no signs of forced entry. No security alert. Whoever did it had time — time to break her, to stage her like art. It was personal. It was precise. And the killer had left no message. No clue.

Just... Renna, like an anatomical exhibit of pain, hanging in silence.

Sol 55 — 09:11

The crew was in shock.

Grace sat wrapped in a blanket, her hands still trembling uncontrollably. Olivia stood beside her, no longer crying, just staring into the floor as if trying to force her mind to believe it had all been imagined. Lar had scrubbed the blood off his hands twice — then again. Then a third time. Each time with more force. Until his palms were raw.

Jonas paced, muttering quietly to himself. "This isn't madness. This is intent. This was methodical. Whoever did that... wanted us to see it."

"We're not dealing with psychosis anymore," Olivia said suddenly, voice flat and cold. "Someone is executing a plan. Step by step. And they want us to come undone."

Lar turned to her, eyes red-rimmed. "It worked."

Sol 55 — 10:33

They tried to examine the scene. Grace fought her nausea long enough to run a scan. There were no fingerprints. No DNA. The surgical wire wasn't from any medkit in the station. The tubing came from the backup oxygen packs — one of which was missing from Supply Closet 3. The killer had planned this well in advance.

More chillingly — the footage from the hallway cams was corrupted.

Every recording between 02:00 and 07:00 showed only static.

Except for one brief flicker.

In the lower corner of one frame: a silhouette. Small. Not muscular. Moving slowly. Then suddenly snapping its head up — as if it saw the camera.

No face.

Just darkness.

Then static again.

And so the truth settled in: they were being hunted by something that knew their routines, their minds, their fear. And Renna... had only been the beginning.

Sol 55 — 10:41

Medical Bay 1 – Autopsy Room

The medbay had never felt colder.

Grace worked with her jaw set and her breathing shallow. She didn't want to be here. But no one else could do this. Not Jonas, whose hands trembled too much. Not Olivia, who hadn't spoken in nearly an hour. And certainly not Lar, who had shut down entirely, a silent figure on the far wall, hugging his knees, muttering something she couldn't hear.

The body had been carefully transported. She'd covered Renna with a sterile sheet, but the outline of her broken limbs still twisted through the fabric like branches beneath ice. Grace had to keep reminding herself: This is about answers. Not guilt. Not grief.

It was when she tried to remove the wire from Renna's mouth that she felt it.

A catch — not just the stitched lips. There was something embedded.

She drew back the wire carefully, and pried the mouth open with the autopsy spreader. The smell was sharp, chemical. And then she saw it: tucked deep behind Renna's teeth, curled like a secret, was a slip of laminated paper.

Tiny. Rolled. Yellowed at the edges.

She pulled it out with forceps, trembling now. Jonas and Olivia stood close. Everyone leaned in.

There was one word, typed in capital letters. It had been folded many times, smudged with blood.

"REMEMBER."

They stared at it in silence. The word sat there, impossibly loud.

Jonas reached out, took it from her hands slowly. He turned it over. There was more.

On the back, in blocky ink:

"THE FIRST WASN'T RENNA. YOU JUST DIDN'T KNOW THEIR NAME."

Olivia flinched, as if struck.

Lar stood, shaking his head slowly. "What does that mean? That there was a murder before the first one? Before Carson?"

Jonas's face was hollow. "Or... maybe it means Carson wasn't the first. Maybe we were already dead before we landed."

Grace backed away from the table. "It's not just a killer anymore. This is someone playing with our reality. They're not just ending lives — they're trying to rewrite what we think we know."

Olivia suddenly turned, walking toward the glass with wide, terrified eyes. Her reflection stared back — pale, gaunt, uncertain.

She whispered, barely audible:

"What if it's not about killing us? What if it's about breaking us so badly... we start to kill each other?"

Feed recording — Not logged in system

A camera still functions. Unknown location.

In the dark, a figure sits cross-legged. We can't see their face.

They hum softly — a tune that sounds familiar, like an old Earth lullaby.

On the floor in front of them: a pile of surgical wire.

And a row of paper scraps, laid out like offerings.

Each says something different:

"THEY LIED ABOUT THE SKY."

"NOT THE FIRST."

"TWO JONASES. NONE REAL."

"SHE OPENED THE DOOR."

"REMEMBER."

The humming stops.

A hand — gloved — picks up a scalpel.

The camera feed ends.

Sol 56 — 06:17
Main Control Room
Lar sat hunched over the station's main console, eyes scanning logs and personnel manifests for anything overlooked. The more he dug, the deeper the pit of unease grew in his chest.

There were... gaps.

Names that appeared briefly in initial crew lists, then disappeared without a trace. Profiles that showed up on internal databases but were wiped clean from mission records. Photos with faces blurred or erased. Records with inconsistent timestamps, as if someone — or something — had tried to scrub their existence from history itself.

He called Olivia over, voice barely steady.

"Look at this," Lar said, pulling up the manifest. "Do you remember these people?" He scrolled through a list of five names, all with positions vital to the mission — engineers, a botanist, a communications specialist. None had ever been mentioned since arrival. No one talked about them, no logs, no messages — as if they were never here.

Olivia's face paled as she scanned the screen. "I don't... I don't remember them. None of it. It's like they were... ghosts."

Jonas appeared behind them, drawn by the tension.

"We should ask the others," he suggested.

Sol 56 — 07:42
Crew Quarters — Group Meeting

The survivors gathered, faces drawn and eyes wary. Lar laid out his findings.

"Does anyone remember working with any of these people?" he asked.

No hands went up.

"I've never seen half of these names," Olivia said quietly.

Jonas frowned. "How can they just vanish? If they were on the mission, we'd know."

Grace looked pale but steady. "Maybe... something happened. Something we don't remember. Or don't want to."

Lar shook his head, heart pounding. "Or someone erased them. From the logs, from our memories. But why? And how?"

Sol 56 — 09:15

Personal Quarters — Olivia's Room

Olivia sat alone, clutching her head. The memories felt like quicksilver — slipping through her fingers every time she tried to hold on. Faces that should have been familiar faded like mist. She saw flashes — a woman's laugh, the rustle of leaves in a greenhouse, a voice whispering in the dark — but no clear picture.

Was it a collective hallucination? Or something worse?

She pulled out a small, worn notebook she'd kept — one place she thought was safe from tampering.

And there, scrawled faintly in the margins:

"They were never meant to stay."

Sol 56 — 11:00

Station Hallway — Jonas Walking

Jonas moved silently through the dim halls, replaying conversations, scanning data terminals for any clue. He stopped at the storage locker — an unmarked, sealed compartment that hadn't been opened since arrival.

His hands trembled as he accessed the keypad. The lock clicked open.

Inside — cold, metallic darkness. But on the floor, faint footprints led to a cluster of faded, dust-covered personal effects: a cracked helmet, a half-burned journal, a photo of a smiling woman he didn't recognize.

His breath caught.

They had been here.

The chilling truth was impossible to deny: there had been others.

But their existence was wiped from time, as though the station itself was erasing its past — including those who had lived, died, or vanished.

And the survivors were left wondering...

Was the killer one of them?

Or something far older, far darker?

The station had grown darker — not just from failing lights, but in the very air, thickening like a shroud.

Lar was the first to speak of it.

At first, it was subtle — fleeting shadows at the edge of vision, whispered sounds just beneath hearing. Olivia dismissed it as exhaustion, but Jonas, ever the skeptic, started doubting his own senses when he caught something moving behind the reinforced glass of the observation deck — a figure that dissolved before he blinked.

Grace felt it too. A cold brush against her neck in empty hallways, her medbay tools shifting inexplicably. The comms started glitching with faint, indecipherable murmurs, sometimes begging, sometimes mocking.

The crew gathered in the central hub, faces pale and voices low.

"It's like... something is here," Lar said, voice cracking. "Not human. Not in any way we know."

Olivia swallowed hard, eyes scanning the dark corners. "But what? How? And why us?"

Jonas frowned, pacing. "We thought the killer was one of us. But what if... they're just a mask? A symptom of something bigger. Something hunting us."

Grace's hands trembled as she clutched her medkit. "If it's here, it's stalking us. Watching us. Testing us."

The presence seemed to toy with them — lights flickered in patterns, doors slammed shut without warning, and the environmental controls briefly plunged parts of the station into freezing darkness.

One night, Lar heard a voice whisper his name through the comms — but when he responded, silence answered back. When Olivia checked the logs, no transmissions had been made.

It was as if the station itself was alive, playing a sinister game.

Jonas discovered strange markings etched beneath the floor panels — symbols that glowed faintly under their flashlights, pulsing like a heartbeat.

"No one made these," he said grimly. "They're old. Alien. And they're spreading."

Olivia's breath caught. "Maybe it's a warning... or a trap."

Paranoia frayed the edges of the crew's sanity. Friends turned wary, eyes darting to shadows that weren't there—or were they?

Grace tried to soothe everyone, but even she began doubting what was real.

One evening, Jonas vanished.

No struggle. No trace.

Only the cold echo of his last words over the comms:

"It's coming. Don't trust the shadows... or each other."

The unseen hunter was no longer a theory. It was a predator.

And the crew were its prey.

The corridors of the station felt colder, darker, and heavier as the unseen presence tightened its grip on the crew. Tension gnawed at every glance, every whispered word. It was into this simmering cauldron that Lisa stepped—a figure sharp and unyielding, her footsteps steady and deliberate.

She had been away on a supply run, a vital mission to salvage parts from the secondary module, but now, with the mounting chaos, her return was more than just a reunion—it was a beacon of hope.

Lisa's eyes scanned the room as she entered the central hub, immediately taking in the strained faces of Lar, Olivia, Grace, and the others. There was no time for greetings or hesitation. "We need to stabilize the comm systems," she said firmly. "If this presence is disrupting our link to Earth, we're blind out here. I'm going to reroute the signal through the old relay arrays."

Her voice cut through the fog of fear, a sharp contrast to the despair hanging thick in the air. She moved with the confidence of someone used to command, yet there was a steel in her gaze that told the others she had faced darkness before—and survived.

Lar nodded, relief flickering in his eyes. "Good. We need that connection, now more than ever."

But even as Lisa set to work, the feeling of being watched clawed at her. Shadows seemed to twist just beyond her vision, and the station's systems flickered unpredictably. Every hum and creak was a reminder: the presence was still here, still hunting.

As Lisa worked tirelessly, the others couldn't help but wonder—was she just the leader they needed, or could she be the next to fall prey to the invisible terror stalking them?

Lisa moved quietly through the dim corridors of the station, her footsteps steady despite the oppressive silence that weighed on everyone. She was the communications specialist, the one who kept their fragile link to Earth alive — or at least tried to. Her sharp eyes missed nothing, and her calm, confident manner gave the others something to cling to amid the spiraling fear.

She found Lar and Olivia in the central hub, their faces etched with exhaustion and suspicion. "Any news?" Lisa asked, her voice low but firm.

Lar shook his head. "The presence... it's still out there. Watching. Waiting."

Olivia's eyes darted nervously to the darkened corners. "It's not just watching. It's playing with us. It's like it knows our fears."

Lisa nodded grimly. "Then we need to stay sharp. I'm rerouting the comms through the secondary arrays — maybe we can get a clean signal, a lifeline."

As she worked, the station's systems flickered violently, the lights dimming and surging like a heartbeat gone mad. A cold draft whispered down the hall, carrying with it a faint, mocking laugh — or maybe just the creak of settling metal. The line between reality and nightmare blurred with every passing second.

Suddenly, Lisa stiffened. Her breath caught. Something unseen brushed past her, colder than Mars itself. A shadow shifted just beyond the reach of her flashlight.

"Did you see that?" she whispered.

Lar's gaze hardened. "It's here. Closer than ever."

In the days that followed, Lisa's presence became a quiet anchor — a reminder that despite the horror hunting them, the crew could still fight back. But the unseen predator was patient. It learned. It waited for the perfect moment.

And that moment was coming.

Understood! Here's the continuation of the story from where we left off—integrating Lisa naturally as part of the crew without disrupting the flow, keeping the tone suspenseful, psychological, and horror-driven, and preserving the focus on the unfolding mystery and mounting terror.

The station's atmosphere had grown unbearably heavy, the silence a choking presence as much as the unseen menace stalking them. Shadows clung to every corner, every hallway, twisting the familiar into something sinister and alien.

Lar moved cautiously through the cramped corridors, his eyes sharp but haunted. Behind him, Olivia and Grace followed closely, the tension between them almost tangible.

Then, from the comm room, came the steady tap of footsteps — firm and purposeful. Lisa emerged, wiping grime from her hands, her gaze scanning the group with a mixture of urgency and calm resolve.

"We need to talk," she said, her voice cutting through the thick fog of dread. "The comms are still unstable. Whatever's out there, it's interfering — not just with our systems, but with us."

Lar nodded, relief mixing with concern. "We're losing time. If we can't reach Earth soon, we're truly isolated."

Lisa's fingers danced over the controls, attempting to reroute signals, but the station's systems flickered erratically — the lights dimming and surging as if responding to some invisible puppeteer.

Suddenly, the bulkhead doors groaned, a metallic scream that echoed through the halls. The crew froze, hearts pounding.

Olivia's voice was barely a whisper. "It's here again."

A sudden crash resounded from the adjacent corridor. The group rushed toward the noise — only to find the passage empty, save for a chilling smear of dark fluid trailing into the shadows.

Lisa crouched, her fingers trembling slightly as she touched the floor. "Blood," she muttered.

Grace swallowed hard. "One of us has been hurt... or worse."

The realization rippled through them. The killer, or whatever hunted them, was escalating.

That night, as the station's emergency lights cast sickly red glows, Lar sat beside the monitors, scanning every feed, every flicker of data for signs of movement. Lisa worked tirelessly to stabilize communications, her usually steady hands betraying a flicker of nervous energy.

In the dark, somewhere beyond their sight, the presence watched, bided its time — while the survivors, battered and broken, clung to the fragile hope that their bonds would outlast the horror closing in.

But as the night deepened, a silent scream echoed through the vent shafts — a sound that promised the nightmare was far from over.

The infirmary was bathed in low amber light, flickering gently with each pulse of the backup generators. The hum of equipment filled the air like a lullaby composed by machines on the edge of death. Grace sat silently beside the medical cot, her fingers clenched into pale fists. Jonas stood at the doorway, shadows swallowing half his face, eyes fixed on the figure lying still beneath a thermal blanket.

Ava.

Her face was gaunt, ghostlike. Streaks of dried blood marked her temples and lips. Deep scratches ran along her collarbone and neck — not random, but deliberate, as if something had carved symbols into her with surgical cruelty. Her breath was shallow, the kind that didn't seem like it belonged to the living.

Then — her eyes opened.

It wasn't sudden, nor theatrical. Just a slow, almost reluctant parting of swollen lids. Her irises flicked left, then right. She did not speak. Her gaze passed over Grace, over Jonas, and stopped at the ceiling — locked there, unblinking.

"Ava?" Grace whispered, leaning closer.

Ava's lips parted. Her voice emerged — hoarse, strangled, like words filtered through gravel.

"Don't turn off the lights."

Jonas moved closer, slowly. "Ava... can you tell us who did this to you?"

Ava didn't respond. Her eyes finally shifted downward — locking onto Jonas. And there, for the briefest moment, he saw it: raw terror. Not directed at something in the room... but at him.

Lisa and Lar were repairing an exposed relay panel in the corridor leading to the vent systems. The station groaned again, metal straining like a tired animal in pain. Olivia stood guard, watching the shadows stretch with each flickering light.

"Jonas hasn't reported in for twenty minutes," Olivia muttered. "And now Ava's awake."

"Think she remembers?" Lisa asked without looking up.

Olivia hesitated. "She was stuffed into a vent. No one survives that and comes back clean."

A loud thud echoed from somewhere above. They froze.

Lisa stood. "That came from the north duct."

They looked up simultaneously.

And for one paralyzing second, they saw it: a shadow inside the ventilation shaft. Motionless. Watching them.

Ava began to convulse. Alarms blared. Grace rushed forward, trying to stabilize her, but Ava's mouth opened wide, and from within — a foreign object fell out.

Jonas caught it before it hit the floor. A tooth.

Not Ava's.

He turned it in his gloved hands. There was a small metal tag attached to the root. Scratched onto it: "J-7" — one of the crew quarters, long sealed off after a systems failure.

Ava stilled. Her eyes rolled back. Her lips trembled with one final whisper.

"He's still in the walls."

The air was dry, metallic, laced with the scent of overheated circuits and old blood. Lar gripped the utility flashlight tighter as he and Lisa followed the narrow maintenance corridor beneath the central comm grid. The shaft was tight — barely wide enough for them to walk side by side. Every few steps, dust rained from the ceiling vents.

"I saw it too, right?" Lisa muttered under her breath, as if needing confirmation. "The shape. In the duct. Watching us."

Lar nodded. "It wasn't a system glitch. That thing had mass. It moved like a person, but slower. Deliberate."

Lisa stopped walking. She stared at a rusted access hatch in the wall — labeled S-9 — its surface warped, dented, almost as if it had been kicked outward.

"Someone's been using the maintenance tunnels," she said. "These aren't on the primary schematics. Not in the new ones anyway."

Lar bent and pried the hatch open. Inside was darkness. Not just lack of light — the kind of thick, crawling dark that felt alive.

"I'll go first," Lar said.

Lisa touched his shoulder. "You sure?"

He gave a half-smile. "No. But let's find out what's crawling in our walls."

He climbed in first, his boots ringing on the steel grating. The shaft beyond was barely shoulder-width, lined with frayed wires and streaks of grime. A faint smell of antiseptic and decay drifted forward — wrongly clean.

Lisa followed, her flashlight darting over twisted pipes and broken panels. One of them was marked with smeared letters — painted hastily, half-erased:

"Do not follow the knocking."

She stopped. "Lar. Look."

He turned and read it silently. His jaw tightened.

Then — a sound. Tap. Tap. Tap.

Both froze.

Tap. Tap. Tap.

It wasn't coming from ahead.

It was coming from above them.

Lisa slowly tilted her head, and there — just behind a loose mesh panel — was a human hand, skeletal, pale, reaching downward. Its fingers tapped rhythmically against the metal.

Lar hissed, stepping back. "Is that—?"

The hand vanished with a sharp jerk, yanked upward.

Lisa's breath trembled. "It knew we were here."

They pushed forward. The shaft opened into a circular junction chamber — a hidden cavity filled with equipment from an older mission era. Dust-covered oxygen tanks. Blank, faded storage crates. And in the center...

A chair.

Straps.

Dried blood.

A broken camera, facing it.

Lisa approached slowly. There was something placed in the center of the chair.

A photo. Water-damaged. Faintly burned.

She lifted it.

Lar leaned in. "Is that—?"

The photo was of the current crew.

All sixteen of them.

Taken on Earth. Before launch.

But behind the row of smiling faces... there was someone else. A blurred figure in the background. No name. No face.

Just a shadow.

Watching.

209

CHAPTER XIII

The Chair Room

The silence in the hidden junction chamber was oppressive — not passive silence, but the kind that waited. Lar stared at the photo in Lisa's trembling hands. Dust floated like ash in the weak beam of his flashlight, and every second dragged heavier than the last.

"I don't remember this photo ever being taken," Lisa whispered. "Do you?"

Lar took it from her, tilting it toward the flickering light.

"No. And this—" he pointed to the blurred figure, "—this isn't a trick of the light. Someone was there."

They turned toward the chair in the middle of the room. The dried blood on the armrests. The gouges in the floor beneath it. The shallow claw marks.

"This place wasn't built for storage," Lisa murmured. "It was built to keep someone in."

Lar walked a slow circle around it, his boot scraping across metal. "A holding chamber."

He reached for the cracked camera mounted above the chair, brushing a layer of grime off the lens. It was smashed inward — not by impact, but almost as if it had exploded from within.

Lisa backed toward one of the sealed storage lockers. "What kind of station was this before we got here?"

Lar didn't answer. He crouched beside the wall, brushing away layers of dust — until he revealed it: an etched number sequence burned into the panel.

Session 83: Subject No. 3— Rejected.

Lisa looked sick. "They were doing experiments down here…"

Suddenly — a loud metallic thud behind them.

They spun around.

A side hatch had closed.

Automatically.

Lisa ran to it, trying to pry it open. "It's sealed — Lar, someone's watching us."

From behind the chair came a low hiss.

Not mechanical.

Breathing.

They froze. Lar aimed his flashlight past the chair, but the beam sputtered.

A shape — hunched, wrongly proportioned — shifted just behind the flickering shadows. The light caught bone-white skin, patches of hair, and something glinting in its hand.

Lar grabbed Lisa's wrist. "Move."

They darted into the side tunnel, slamming the manual override and sprinting through the narrow crawlspace. Behind them — the sound of scratching on metal followed, then the knocking again.

Tap. Tap. Tap.

Tap. Tap. Tap.

As if mocking their footfalls.

In the infirmary, Ava sat upright, eyes blank, whispering to herself.

Grace turned sharply. "Ava?"

Ava didn't respond to her name. Instead, she repeated a phrase under her breath:

"Three left behind. Three left behind. But it only ever needed one to open the door."

Jonas stepped forward. "What door?"

Ava finally looked up — not at them, but through them.

"The one you've already walked through."

The corridor was too narrow, and the walls felt like they were closing in. Lar's boots slammed against the grated floor with a rhythm driven by pure adrenaline. Lisa was right behind him, breath ragged, still holding the burned photo in her clenched fist.

When they finally burst into the light of the central deck, Jonas was already there, gun raised instinctively — though the moment he saw them, his expression shifted from suspicion to cold shock.

"Where the hell have you been?" Jonas barked.

Grace, beside him, stepped forward, concern shadowing her features. "You're both filthy. What happened?"

Lar barely caught his breath before replying.

"There's... there's a hidden chamber under the comms grid. It's not on any blueprint."

Lisa cut in. "A chair. Blood. Someone was strapped down. There's... a photo. Of us. From Earth."

Olivia stood from the terminal. "What are you talking about?"

Lisa handed over the burned image.

As Olivia studied it, the blood drained from her face. "This was taken in Houston. But there's someone else in the background."

"Exactly," Lar said. "Someone not part of the crew manifest. Watching us, before we even launched."

Jonas narrowed his eyes. "You're saying... someone followed us here?"

Lar hesitated. "Or was here before us."

That silenced the room.

Grace looked around nervously. "Where's Elias?"

"Still missing," Jonas muttered. "And now Ava's repeating gibberish about a door."

Lisa rubbed her temples. "There was... something down there. Not just a place. A presence. It moved in the dark."

"No," Lar said, barely above a whisper. "It stalked us."

Everyone fell into a cold, collective silence.

Then—

Tap. Tap. Tap.

The sound came from the overhead duct above them.

Jonas turned, aiming his weapon at the grating.

Everyone backed away from beneath it.

The tapping stopped.

Grace whispered, "Where's Renna?"

No one answered.

They pried open the supply room door. A faint trail of blood smeared along the floor tiles, leading toward the storage unit.

Jonas pulled the hatch open slowly.

Nothing inside.

Just one thing.

A set of bloody teeth, set neatly in a straight line on the floor — Renna's dental caps.

Lisa turned away and vomited. Grace fell against the wall, shaking.

Olivia stared at the line of teeth and murmured:

"This thing isn't just killing us. It's... playing."

It was just after the lights flickered — just once, and not in any scheduled cycle. Olivia had been scanning security feeds for hours, trying to stitch together anything coherent, any sign of who or what was hunting them. Lisa paced silently near the airlock, knuckles white around the grip of a wrench.

Lar was whispering with Grace in the corner, his voice low and tight, the air between them thick with fear and something unspoken. Jonas, still blood-streaked from the last recovery, sat in silence beside Ava, whose eyes remained locked on the same corner of the wall, lips muttering fragments of a nursery rhyme.

Then came the alert.

External sensor breach — Airlock 3.

Everyone froze.

Olivia spun toward the console. "No one went out there. We sealed it."

Grace stood. "Check the feed."

Static.

For the first time in hours, Ava blinked. Then said, without turning:

"He's back."

The hatch to Airlock 3 hissed.

A shape stepped through, hunched, backlit by the emergency lights.

Elias.

But not Elias.

His suit was torn — as though he'd clawed his way out of something far too tight. His helmet hung in one hand. The side of his face bore an old wound — stitched crudely shut — that none of them remembered him having before.

His eyes were distant. Bloodshot. Tracking things that weren't there.

He stopped just inside the threshold.

No one moved.

Lar was the first to speak.

"Elias?"

He looked up. Blinked.

"I saw you," Elias whispered.

Lisa stepped back. "What?"

"I saw you... before you saw me. You were already here."

He walked forward — slow, deliberate. Everyone stood frozen, unsure whether to run or reach for a weapon.

Elias's eyes drifted over to Jonas.

"You opened the door, didn't you?"

"What door?" Jonas asked quietly.

Elias just smiled. It was the most wrong smile any of them had ever seen.

Grace checked Elias's vitals. They were... normal. His blood pressure steady. No signs of trauma — not the kind science could explain.

But then she found it: carved into the inside of his left arm, hidden under gauze, were letters — not just cut into flesh, but burned in:

"REMEMBER WHO YOU WERE."

Grace stepped back.

Elias looked at her and smiled again.

"Do you know what you've done yet?" he asked.

They put Elias in the Containment Module — a small, sealed bay originally meant for contaminated samples. Its walls were reinforced, transparent, and coldly clinical. There was a moment — just one — where he looked up at them through the glass, eyes searching each face with something that almost resembled pity.

Jonas, arms folded tight across his chest, wouldn't look at him.

Lisa lingered, her face unreadable.

Lar secured the outer lock.

"Keep him in there," Olivia muttered. "No matter what he says."

Grace remained behind. She stood there for too long, watching Elias sit cross-legged in the center of the room. He didn't speak. Didn't beg. Just watched her with tired, knowing eyes.

"He needs help," she whispered to herself.

He heard her.

"I tried to warn you," he said, voice barely muffled by the glass. "I tried before they came."

Grace froze. "They?"

"The ones who wake up when we remember too much."

Lisa and Lar were double-checking the locks on the lower sectors when the lights cut out.

Just a flicker.

But when they came back on, the door to the hydroponic bay was slightly ajar — even though it had been sealed since Day 12.

Jonas was the one who found the message, scrawled in soil across the greenhouse wall, letters uneven, almost frantic:

"He is not the first. You were never the first."

Underneath the words was a pile of dried, flattened uniforms — the kind issued at launch. But these weren't theirs. The crew manifest on the chest tags had unfamiliar names. Four of them.

And in the center of the pile: a fresh, bloodied scalpel.

Containment Room, 1 Hour Later

Grace returned to check on Elias.

He was still sitting, still quiet.

But behind him — on the transparent wall — were dozens of handprints.

Pressed from the inside.

Elias turned slowly, smiling.

"It's not me you should be afraid of anymore."

The cold had returned — not the kind that tickled the skin but the kind that seeped into the bones of the station. No one spoke of it, but everyone felt it. Something had shifted since Elias's return. Even the air tasted wrong.

Jonas sat by the security console, eyes flicking from one grainy cam feed to the next. Every shadow stretched too long. Every noise — every distant hiss of the vents — made his spine tighten.

Olivia and Grace were in MedBay, reviewing the old scans — ones from before the first death. Trying to find patterns. Consistencies. There were none.

Lar and Lisa checked the hydroponics again. The uniforms were still there, untouched — except one. Now, a single set was missing. Neither of them mentioned it.

Ava was asleep — or pretending to be — curled up in the far corner of the rec room, muttering to herself again, voice low and rhythmic.

Then the power flickered.

Only for a second.

But it was enough.

A scream tore through the intercom.

Raw. Human. Terrified.

It echoed from the engineering deck — the place they had sealed two days ago.

Jonas was the first to move, weapon raised, heart pounding. Lar and Lisa were right behind him.

They weren't fast enough.

The first thing they noticed was the smell — acrid, metallic, something that clung to the back of the throat.

Then they saw the blood.

It was pooled beneath the main coolant chamber — in gallons. And something else was pooled there too: long, curling strips of skin. Peeled, almost surgically. Each one was nailed to the wall with makeshift metal pins, forming an intricate, spiral pattern.

Grace turned and covered her mouth, stifling a scream.

Olivia whispered, "Where's Ava?"

They found her.

Or parts of her.

Her body — or what was left of it — hung from the ceiling, suspended by a tangle of electrical wire and tubing. Her jaw was torn nearly off, and her eyes were gone, replaced by small black pebbles — glassy and smooth.

On her chest, carved with cruel precision, were the words:

"OFFERING ACCEPTED."

Lisa stumbled back, hyperventilating. Lar pulled her away as Jonas dropped to his knees, staring blankly.

Olivia looked up, horrified. "He's in the cell. He couldn't have—"

Then Lar said it. Quiet, but certain:

"Unless it's not just one of us."

Back in the control deck, the others stared at the footage.

The feed from the engineering corridor was corrupted. But one frame — one single, unglitched frame — remained.

A figure in the distance.

Not Ava.

Not Elias.

Not anyone they recognized.

The body was tall, and thin, face blurred. It was wearing the missing uniform from the hydroponics pile.

And in its hand — a long, bloodied blade.

Jonas whispered, "That's not possible."

Lisa turned toward him slowly.

"What if... we're not alone?"

They stood around the shaft like mourners at a grave. The silence between them was not indecision — it was dread. No one spoke because speaking would make it real. The fact that it was deeper than the schematics showed, that it swallowed light like a throat.

Lisa was the first to move. She strapped herself to the climb harness and said nothing. No motivational speech, no glance back.

Jonas followed, then Lar. Grace went last, her eyes sweeping the dark corridor as if expecting it to vanish the moment she turned away.

The shaft was warm. Breathing.

The air got thicker as they descended, as though they were climbing down into something living. At thirty meters, the steel gave way to rusted iron. The rungs felt older, worn down — though by what, none of them could say.

There were no insects on Mars. No mold. No moisture.

And yet there was rot.

Jonas hit the bottom first, flashlight trembling in his hand. He swept the beam across the chamber.

The floor was identical to the observation deck above. Same tiles, same angles, same faded stripes. A perfect replica.

Grace landed beside him. "Jonas," she whispered. "Is that..."

"Yes."

On the far wall was a terminal. Old, dusty. Powered off.

But as they approached — it powered on by itself.

The screen blinked:

WELCOME BACK, DR. GRACE YOUNG.

Grace took a step back. "I never... I never signed into anything here."

Jonas scrolled through the files.

There were dozens. All names from the team. All labeled:

CYCLE COMPLETE

TRIGGER ACCEPTED

LOCK RESET

And one more:

SUBJECT #07: GRACE YOUNG — TRIGGER DENIED

Her hand shook as she reached out and opened the file.

Inside: recordings. One was labeled "THERAPY SIMULATION — PHASE 3"

Grace's own voice filled the room. Calm. Collected. Clinical.

"Let's run the dream again. The corridor, the dripping sound, the knife in your hand. This time, let it play through..."

She staggered back, horrified.

"I never said that! That isn't me!"

Jonas looked to the side — saw Lar stiffen as he opened his own file.

He was staring at a video still.

It was himself.

Standing in a room covered in blood.

Smiling.

The timestamp read six months before launch.

Above, Olivia heard the whisper again.

It came from the console room, down the hall she had already cleared twice.

"Come see..."

She stepped forward, breath shallow, flashlight flickering.

She passed the broken camera — and the monitor next to it turned on. Just static.

Then:

A frame of her, standing in the same room, watching the same screen — but her eyes were bleeding.

Back in the chamber

Grace fell to her knees, overwhelmed. "They lied to us," she said. "This was never about building a colony. This was—this was a test."

Jonas backed away, his own heart hammering. "A test for what?"

Lar turned, dead serious.

"A test to see if we could become killers."

Grace sat on the floor, knees pulled up to her chest, the light from the terminal screen flickering across her face. Jonas crouched nearby, watching her hands tremble as she played the audio again.

"Corridor, dripping sound, knife in your hand…"

Every time she heard it, her expression tightened — but her eyes held something else now. Not just fear.

Recognition.

Jonas hadn't said anything yet. He couldn't. He kept seeing the image from Lar's terminal: Lar's face, bathed in blood, not screaming, not crying — just smiling with eyes void of anything human.

But Lar stood behind them now, pacing the edge of the chamber like a man trying not to scream.

"I don't remember anything like this," he said, more to himself than anyone else. "I've never—never seen that place. I've never killed anyone."

No one answered him.

They couldn't.

Because what if he wasn't the only one?

Grace finally looked up, her voice raw. "Jonas, I've had dreams. Of… knives. Of rooms with red walls. I thought they were stressed. Nightmares. But what if—" She paused, shivering. "What if they're memories?"

Jonas didn't know what scared him more: that it might be true… or that he didn't remember his dreams.

He looked back at the terminal.

The log entries had timestamps. One every twenty days.

Each labeled:

"TRIGGER ENABLED — MEMORY WIPED"

All but one:

"JONAS REED: INCOMPLETE TRIGGER — RETENTION POSSIBLE"

His hands clenched.
What did that mean?
Then the lights flickered.
Just once.
But long enough to throw their shadows against the wall in strange, contorted forms.
The screen turned black.
A single sentence appeared:
"She remembers now. Do you?"

Jonas stood so fast his chair clattered to the floor.
"Lar," he said. "Get Olivia. Now."
But Lar didn't move.
He was staring at the wall, expression blank.
"What's wrong?" Jonas asked.
Lar lifted his hand, slowly pointing toward the far side of the room.
There was another door. A narrow seam where no blueprint said there should be anything.
And a trail of wet footprints leading into it.
They weren't alone.

Meanwhile, above
Olivia stood in the comms room, arms folded, watching the static pulse on the monitor.
A voice crackled through the feed — not the system, not the comms.

A whisper.

Her own.

"We already did this, remember?"

She staggered back, her vision suddenly splitting — the screen showing not one image, but two. In one, she was sitting calmly, typing a report. In the other, she was beating something against the wall.

The split lasted less than a second.

But her hands were already shaking.

Behind her, Ava stepped into the room quietly, her eyes rimmed red from exhaustion.

"You alright?"

Olivia turned too fast. "Yeah. Just—" She paused. "...Just tired."

Ava nodded. "I've been dreaming of a mirror room. And something inside me. Clawing."

Olivia didn't speak.

Because she'd been dreaming the same thing.

The scream tore through the station like a ragged blade. Olivia was the first to hear it — distant, shrill, sharp enough to make her drop the coffee tin she was holding. It rolled across the floor, spinning in a circle before falling still.

She ran.

Grace was already in the hall by the time Olivia arrived, pale and wide-eyed. Behind her, Lar sprinted in silence, his jaw clenched tight.

They followed the sound to Sector C.

The maintenance corridor. The one with the lights that never worked right.

The air felt too warm.

The door to the old solar relay room was ajar. Something wet smeared across its surface.

Lar pushed it open.

They saw her at the same time.

Lisa.

Hanging from the ceiling like a marionette, her neck bent completely backwards, head twisted at an impossible angle. Her eyes were wide open, frozen in an expression that no one could quite describe. It was as if she had seen something not just terrifying — but profoundly wrong.

Her hands were shredded.

Not cut.

Shredded — as though she had clawed something for hours.

Blood had been used to draw something on the wall behind her.

A mirror. A crude one.

Just a rectangle with a face staring back from it — her own, smiling. The rest of the wall was covered in bloody smears. Words written over and over again:

"SHE LOOKED FIRST"

"SHE LOOKED FIRST"

"SHE LOOKED FIRST"

Grace gasped and covered her mouth.

Olivia turned to look away — and caught a reflection in the broken vent panel behind them.

It looked like Jonas.

Just for a second.

But when she spun around — he wasn't there.

Elsewhere

Jonas was in the reactor corridor, alone.

He'd found something hours earlier. A fragment of a recording, left in a locked folder. One Grace had tried to open and failed.

He had seen a few seconds of it.

Elias, standing in the mirror room. Crying. Whispering:

"I didn't want to... I didn't know I did it..."

Then a flicker.

And Jonas had seen himself — same room — smiling.

He hadn't told anyone yet. Not even Grace.

Because something in him didn't want to know more.

Not yet.

Back at the body, Lar stared at Lisa's corpse and said nothing. But Olivia noticed something. A detail that slipped past the others.

Her boots.

One of them was missing.

No blood trail.

No shoe anywhere in sight.

Just the print of a single barefoot... walking into the dark.

Grace couldn't sleep.

She sat curled in the dim-lit medbay, eyes tracing the edge of the terminal screen, though the screen had long since gone dark. Her hands wouldn't stop shaking. Her mind wouldn't stop repeating.

Lisa's face.

That backward-bent neck.

The words in blood.

The missing boot.

But it wasn't just the horror.

It was Jonas's absence.

He'd vanished just before the body was found. Reappeared hours later — pale, silent, sweating — claiming he'd been fixing a breach alert in Sector F. But there was no breach alert. Grace had checked.

And worse — she'd seen the fragment.

The recording Jonas had hidden from her.

She replayed it again now, earphones pressed tight to her skull. Elias in the mirror room, weeping. Whispering.

"I didn't want to... I didn't know I did it..."

But it was the final frame — corrupted, but visible — that made her insides coil like a noose tightening.

Jonas.

Standing in the same place.

The same smile.

She hadn't told anyone. She didn't know if it was real. Or a hallucination. Or a fabrication stitched into her mind like a virus.

But the bloodied messages.

The unpredictable blackouts.

The feeling that the base itself remembered more than they did...

She couldn't ignore it anymore.

So when Jonas entered the room, she didn't turn to greet him.

He paused, watching her.

"You're awake."

"So are you," she said.

He gave her a weak smile. "No one's sleeping tonight."

Grace didn't smile back. "Where were you, Jonas? Before they found Lisa?"

He frowned, defensive. "I told you. Reactor corridor. I thought the breach—"

"There was no breach."

Silence.

She stood now, slowly, her voice soft but cold. "I checked the logs. There was no breach, no alert, no repair order. You were gone for three hours."

Jonas looked away.

She took a step closer. "Why didn't you tell me about the file?"

He didn't answer.

"Jonas," she said. "I saw it. The video. You were there. The mirror room."

Still nothing. Just the faintest twitch in his jaw.

Grace wanted to stop. She wanted to believe in him — needed to believe. But something deep in her core — something primal and ancient — was warning her:

> He's not telling you everything.

"You have to tell me the truth," she said. "Because if you don't... I don't know if I can protect you."

Jonas's eyes flicked to hers now.

Not angry.

But scared.

"Grace," he whispered. "What if it wasn't me?"

She stared at him.

"Then who?" she asked.

He didn't answer. Just looked past her — toward the glass reflection on the darkened console. And for a heartbeat, Grace thought she saw movement in that reflection.

A flicker.

A face.

Not Jonas.

Something wearing his skin.

Lar had never been afraid of silence.

It had been his companion since childhood — in empty fields, beneath stars, within the claustrophobic stillness of his first spacewalk. But now... the silence inside the southern wing felt wrong.

Too still.

Too deliberate.

Too quiet.

He walked carefully through the corridor, his boots echoing over steel grates dusted with ash and debris. This part of the base had been closed after the first breach. Supposedly sealed. But the hatch had been unlocked when he checked it tonight.

Something had drawn him here. A hum in his bones. An itch behind his teeth.

A few hours earlier, he'd been searching old logs — not files, not video. He'd given up on those. They were all corrupt. He was looking for manual prints — schematics left in physical archive.

What he found...

A map of the base.

But not their base.

Not exactly.

The layout was wrong. There were extra rooms. Hidden corridors. An entire sublevel below their own. There was no mention of it in the briefings. Nothing in their walkthroughs.

The print was dated eight years before their mission began.

Someone had been here before.

Or maybe... something still was.

And now, standing at the end of the hall, Lar saw the proof.

A sealed door, blinking faintly with green status lights. No one had used it in months. Years. But the panel was warm.

He pried it open and stepped inside.

The room was small.

Dustless.

Cold.

Metal walls gleamed with surgical precision. A chair sat in the center — not a normal one — a restraint chair. Heavy straps. A head clamp. Dried brown stains around the seams.

A glass partition split the room from another.

On the other side: mirrors. Cameras. Observation equipment.

And taped to one of the mirrors — photos.

Fifteen of them.

Every member of the current trent crew.

Except for one photo.

Lar's own.

It had been scratched out — deep gouges through his face, eyes removed. Beside it: a single word written in sharp ink.

"IMMUNE?"

Lar's mouth went dry. He stepped back — heart pounding now.

Something else was on the floor. A recorder. He picked it up, clicked play.

Static hissed, then a voice. Raspy. Familiar. His own.

"They're watching us. Not just the ones we see. Something crawled inside. It wears us. Mirrors are wrong — don't look too long. Don't look or it notices you. God help the ones it notices..."

The recording cut.

Lar dropped it. Backed away.

He turned — only to find the mirror staring back.

But his reflection didn't match his movement.

It smiled.

Lar's breath hitched.

Behind him, the room fell completely dark.

Grace was tired of hearing her own heartbeat.

It thudded constantly in her ears now — ever since Lisa's body had been found with her jaw dislocated and one boot missing, her face still frozen in an expression Grace saw every time she blinked.

Now, in the soft light of the small hydroponics lab — one of the few places not soaked in blood or panic — Grace and Jonas sat, sipping the last of the warm nutrient liquid. It almost felt like soup. It almost felt human.

"I keep thinking," Grace said finally, "that maybe it's all some kind of contamination. Air-borne. A parasite. Something that's... changing us. What if none of us are really us anymore?"

Jonas didn't answer immediately. His hands were wrapped around the metal cup, but he hadn't taken a sip. He looked at her, searching her eyes.

"I've been thinking the same thing," he said. "But what if the parasite... isn't in the air?"

"What do you mean?"

He set the cup down. "What if it's in our heads? In our memories? What if it's rewriting things we thought we knew?"

Grace leaned back slightly. She hated how easily those words fit into the puzzle forming in her mind.

Jonas continued, "I remember being in the comms room when Ava died. I remember that. But now I'm not sure if I actually was. I only know that I remember it that way. What if that memory was given to me?"

She swallowed hard. "So you think someone is manipulating us?"

"Someone... or something."

A long silence stretched between them.

Grace reached across the table, slowly, taking his hand. "I want to believe you," she said. "I want to believe we can still trust each other."

Jonas's eyes softened — grateful, but hollow. "I want to trust myself too."

She noticed something then — a faint, jagged scar at the base of his neck. She hadn't seen it before. Thin, almost surgical. She reached toward it without thinking.

"Jonas, what is this?"

He touched it as if noticing it for the first time. "I... I don't know. I don't remember getting hurt."

Grace's breath hitched.

Then suddenly — the comm crackled to life.

A voice. Distorted. Faint. Not Lar's. Not Olivia's.

It sounded like Elias.

"You shouldn't be together. It watches when you're together. It listens through reflections. Don't look in the glass. Don't—"

Static.

Then silence.

Jonas and Grace stared at each other.

Grace stood. "We need to find Lar."

Jonas nodded slowly. "And Elias... if that was really him."

But something in both their faces had changed. A small, invisible fracture had formed.

Because they both knew — if memories weren't real, then neither of them could truly know who the other was.

And the mirrors in the lab?

One of them had just fogged over.

But neither had breathed near it.

CHAPTER XIV

The Seventeen Face

Olivia couldn't hear her own breathing anymore. It was buried beneath the metallic whine of the corridor walls — like the station itself was exhaling through its seams. Something in her mind was cracking, like old paint curling off a forgotten door.

She was alone. Or supposed to be.

She'd followed the streaks. They weren't just blood — there were scrapes, too. Long gouges in the floor panels leading away from the lab. Like someone had been dragged, or worse — clawed backward.

Lar had vanished. No body. No sound. Just his commlink left blinking softly on the floor, still warm when she'd found it.

Now she stood outside one of the unused habitation pods — Pod 11, sealed months ago due to a malfunction in its oxygen stabilizers. The door had a handprint smeared on it in something that had dried to black. Not blood. Something thicker.

Inside, the light flickered weakly — the emergency battery long past its recommended limits. Olivia entered, slow as if walking into a tomb, and then she saw it.

A message, scratched into the mirror on the far wall — faint, like it had been written with a fingernail.

"We were never alone. Not even before. It was always one of us."

– L

Her throat tightened. She blinked. Was that Lar's voice in her head? Was it memory? Madness?

She moved closer.

There, behind the mirror — a sliver of something folded into the seam. A torn piece of fabric. Blue. Regulation uniform. She pulled it free, revealing something pressed into it: a data crystal. Her hands shook as she inserted it into her portable unit.

The video began. Blurry, soundless at first. Then came the static, and Lar's face filled the frame. He looked terrified. Hunched. Whispers bled into the audio.

"They're wrong. About everything. About the logs. The system time is a lie — they reset us. I found footage of Jonas... of me. Of things I don't remember doing."

He looked offscreen, eyes wide.

"It isn't all hallucinations. It's the structure. There are levels beneath. I heard breathing down there. It wasn't human."

Static. Then screaming. Something metal. The screen went black.

And that was it.

Olivia stumbled backward. Something about that scream — it didn't belong to Lar.

It belonged to her. She remembered that pitch. That terror. She had screamed like that in a dream — or had it been real?

Was she also losing pieces of herself?

The mirror behind her began to fog — but the temperature in the room hadn't changed.

Her reflection stayed still for one second too long.

Grace stood in the medbay, elbows pressed to the sterile counter, her reflection staring back from a surgical cabinet's glass pane. She hadn't slept. Not really. Just fragments of dreamless dark, blinking in and out like broken film.

Jonas was somewhere behind her, quiet. Too quiet.

She'd noticed it — how he avoided mirrors now. Not overtly. Just slight shifts in his movement, subtle hesitations when walking past reflective surfaces. Like he didn't trust what he might see.

"You okay?" she finally asked, voice low, unsure if she was asking him or herself.

He didn't answer right away. Then:

"I think... someone's watching us through them."

Grace turned to him slowly. "Mirrors?"

He nodded. "Not just mirrors. Screens. Even the polished panels. They're showing things that... they shouldn't. My reflection — it smiled at me last night. I wasn't smiling."

She felt her stomach twist. This was how it started — with tiny fractures in perception. And they were surrounded by glass, metal, and endless surfaces.

Jonas walked to the far wall and wiped the dust from a rarely used monitor. It flickered on by itself.

A still image appeared. A hallway. Narrow. Familiar. But... wrong.

There were two of him.

One in the frame, walking past. Another standing still, watching. The second Jonas didn't blink.

"I didn't do this," he whispered.

Grace reached for the terminal's shutdown switch but froze. Carved into the plastic casing, deep and deliberate, were words:

"WATCH WHO WATCHES."

She yanked the power, and the image vanished. Silence. Then the door behind them slammed shut.

Automatic. They were locked in.

From the speakers overhead, soft static bled in. Then something else. Not music. Not language.

Breathing.

Grace backed into Jonas, trembling.

"It's us," she said. "Something's mimicking us."

He didn't respond. He was staring at the window on the door.

Two shadows stood outside.

Then one disappeared — but no footsteps.

The door unlocked with a slow hiss. They didn't open it. Just stood there. Hearts pounding.

And on the floor, where nothing had been before, lay a photo.

Not a printout. A real photograph.

It showed the crew. The full crew. Sixteen of them.

But there were seventeen people in the picture.

The last figure — obscured at the edge, face blurry — had no reflection in the mirrored console behind them.

Jonas held the photograph like it was an infected thing. The edges curled slightly, the surface cold despite the room's heavy heat. Grace leaned in, inspecting the shadows, the faces, counting again and again as if numbers might change if whispered gently.

"Seventeen," she said finally. "There were never seventeen of us."

"No," Jonas replied. "But someone wanted us to believe there were."

He turned the photo over. Nothing on the back. But he could feel something — like a presence pressing through it, a memory that didn't belong to him.

Grace took the image and placed it beneath a sterilizer's magnifier. The light washed over the photo, revealing smudges invisible to the naked eye.

"Wait—" she said sharply.

There was faint ink. Barely legible.

"WE WERE NEVER SIXTEEN."

The word "never" was underlined — several times, deep enough to have almost torn the paper.

Jonas stepped back. "Grace... Do you remember the arrival manifest? The launch?"

"I've memorized every crew member's profile," she said quietly. "And none of them looked like this." She pointed to the blurred figure at the edge of the photo.

He was half-turned, his head low. Not a glitch or motion blur — more like the photo had actively resisted capturing him. His uniform had no nameplate. No country emblem. Just blank fabric.

Grace's voice dropped.

"Look at the position of his hands."

Jonas squinted. One hand rested on a crewmate's shoulder. The other... wasn't right. Too long. Too thin. Fingers like they had too many joints.

Neither of them spoke for a long moment.

Then Jonas turned to the nearest terminal and began to dig through archived footage — even though he had sworn he wouldn't do that again. The files had been corrupted so many times, tampered with. But this time, Grace helped him bypass the deeper security layers. A private log appeared. Dated before launch. Not accessible to crew.

A feed of the launch prep room.

Jonas leaned in as figures passed the camera — technicians, pilots, scientists.

And there — for half a second — was the same blurry man. Same height. Same build. Passing through the edge of the frame, face turned.

"Do you see that?" Jonas whispered.

Grace stared. "Why is he... why is he always just barely seen?"

But it got worse.

As the log continued, the man appeared again. This time closer. In the background of the crew photo session. Again, in the mess hall during a meal. Then again. And again.

Always in the background.

And always one more than there should be.

Jonas shut the terminal. "This isn't just someone who came with us."

Grace's voice was tight, almost hollow. "What if he's not someone at all?"

They sat in silence. Then a soft chime — the motion detector by the door blinked. A shadow moved past.

Jonas opened the door slowly, and found nothing.

Except one thing.

A fresh photo. Clipped to the doorframe.

It was taken from behind them, from inside the room.

They turned back. The room was empty. But behind the surgical curtain, a shape shifted — too tall to be either of them. The curtain fluttered once.

And then went still.

The curtain didn't move again.

It just hung there, sterile white, soft as breath — like it hadn't just flickered from something tall brushing against it.

Jonas stood frozen, the photo still in his hand, his heartbeat loud enough that he could feel it behind his teeth. Grace was behind him, one step back, her hand subtly reaching for the surgical scalpel on the nearby tray.

Jonas forced a breath into his lungs.

"I'm going to pull it," he said, voice thin.

"No," Grace murmured, her voice like paper tearing. "Not yet. Think. Whatever was here took a photo of us. From behind. That means it was already in the room... while we were facing the door."

The air felt heavier suddenly. Denser. A pressure in the ears, like being too deep underwater.

Jonas moved slowly toward the curtain, his fingers trembling as he reached for the edge of the fabric.

He yanked it aside.

Nothing.

No figure. No threat. No monster.

Just shadows.

Just silence.

But the floor tile behind the curtain was wet — a smear of something dark and sticky. Not blood. It was thicker. Black. Like crude oil mixed with ash. And at the center of the stain, a perfect footprint.

Five toes.

But far too long. And wide. Not human.

Grace bent to inspect it, her nose wrinkling as the smell hit her — copper and mold. "Jonas..."

He already knew. "It's not ours."

Something moved in the ceiling.

They both looked up at once. The air vent was slowly rotating — turning as if something inside it had crawled too far and disturbed the mechanism. A faint scraping echoed through the ducts. A dragging sound. Nails or bone.

Jonas reached the terminal and opened the environmental schematic of their sector. "These vents connect to half the station," he whispered. "If something's moving through them..."

He didn't finish.

Because then the terminal blinked — not in a glitch, but like something had overridden it.

The screen turned black.

And then white letters typed themselves across it:

"IT IS INSIDE ALL OF YOU."

"ONLY ONE WILL LEAVE."

The power cut out.

Total blackout.

Jonas reached for Grace. "Don't move. Don't—"

But a distant scream tore through the vents. It wasn't just human — it was multiple voices, layered over each other, like a chorus of distorted recordings being played backwards.

They turned to run.

But the door wouldn't open.

And in the mirror cabinet on the far wall, the two of them were still standing still.

Even though they were now across the room.

Jonas stared into the reflection, and his knees went weak.

In the mirror, he blinked — but the mirrored Grace didn't.

Instead, her reflection smiled. Slowly. A knowing, inhuman grin.

Then lifted a hand and pointed — behind them.

They turned.

And the curtain had returned to its closed position.

Grace stepped forward and tore it back again.

This time — there was something.

Something left behind.

Not a person.

A mass of skin. Not shaped. Not connected to bone. Just peeled flesh, hanging like an abandoned coat.

Inside it, a name tag floated, soaked through:

RENNER — BIOCOMM TECH.

Jonas stumbled back, bile rising in his throat. He'd seen Renner three days ago. Alive. Working on DNA sequencing. Quiet. Distant.

But now... she'd been emptied out. As if something had worn her. And then shed her.

Grace knelt over it, whispering in disbelief. "Someone... something's copying us."

"Or wearing us," Jonas said hoarsely.

Then the lights above flickered back on.

The reflection now showed only one person.

Just Jonas.

Grace was no longer in the mirror.

But she was still beside him.

Looking just as terrified as he felt.

The hallway was wrong.

Jonas knew it the moment they stepped out of the infirmary. The architecture was identical — same sharp corners, same strip-lighting — but something about the shadows was off. The light didn't bend the way it should. The far end of the corridor looked too far. The walls hummed with a low vibration, barely perceptible, like the entire structure was alive and breathing slowly.

Grace walked ahead, holding a flashlight she didn't remember picking up.

"This corridor wasn't here before," she said. "I know every hallway in this wing."

Jonas nodded. "I've lived here for over a year. This isn't part of it."

They reached the end, where the hallway split — but instead of the familiar right and left passageways, there was a single black door. No markings. No panel. Just matte steel and the sense that something behind it was listening.

Grace reached out.

The door clicked.

And opened.

They stepped through—

—and were somewhere else.

A vast, circular chamber. White. Clean. Blinding lights overhead. Monitors lined the walls, but the feeds were static — except for one: it played footage from the launch bay, years ago. Their own launch. But the angles were impossible. From inside sealed rooms, from the cockpit mid-flight, from inside their helmets.

Jonas whispered, "How are these even recorded?"

A voice answered.

"Because we never left."

They both turned, violently.

Lar stood there, panting, bruised, Lisa right behind him — her face streaked with blood, her eyes wide and trembling. They looked like they had run through something on fire.

"What—what do you mean?" Grace asked.

Lisa was the one who spoke. "We found... something. Beneath Engineering. A whole level that wasn't on the blueprints. A lab. A... goddamn theatre. Cameras. Feeding into this."

She pointed to the monitors.

Jonas walked closer to the one showing his own helmet feed. He saw himself, on Day 2 of the mission, drinking from his hydration pack, talking casually. But the audio was wrong.

The voice on the video wasn't his.

It sounded like him. Looked like him.

But it spoke different words.

"I've already chosen the next one. She won't fight. They never do when I say their name."

Grace stepped back.

Lisa moved to the central console. Her hands were shaking. "There's a record here — names, dates, logs of 'interventions'. I don't think this was a mission. I think we were put here."

Lar, silent until now, finally spoke.

"There are sixteen logs. One for each of us."

He turned to the others. "But a seventeenth file just unlocked when we entered."

Jonas approached the console. The log file flickered open, displaying a name he didn't recognize.

SUBJECT-17: ENTITY

STATUS: OBSERVING / MIGRATORY

CURRENT FORM: UNKNOWN

HOST BONDING: SUCCESSFUL

OBJECTIVE: FINAL ACT COMMENCING

Grace backed away from the console. "What the hell does that mean?"

Then every screen blinked.

The video feeds went black.

A countdown appeared across all of them.

00:10

00:09

Lisa yelled, "It's a purge."

00:08

Lar grabbed Grace. "MOVE!"

They ran back to the door — but it had vanished. There was no exit. Just walls.

00:06

00:05

Jonas looked up — the ceiling now slowly descending.

It wasn't mechanical. It was... soft. Like skin stretching, pulling downward with bone under it. Faces pressing outward from behind the surface.

Not screaming.

Smiling.

00:03

Jonas grabbed the central console and ripped the wires from the panel. Sparks exploded — and the lights blew out.

Darkness.

But the countdown stopped.

Silence.

Then a voice — not from the comms. Not from the walls.

From inside their skulls.

"ONLY ONE WILL REMEMBER."

Lisa was gone.

So was Lar.

Grace gripped Jonas' arm. "Did we black out? Or—?"

Then they heard it.

A faint dragging sound behind the wall.

And the voice of Lisa.

But her words were garbled. Choked. Like her throat had been filled with liquid.

Jonas put a hand to the wall.

It was warm.

And beating.

Grace spoke, brokenly. "This base is not what we thought it was."

Jonas whispered, "It's not even a base anymore."

They turned to each other, understanding slowly dawning.

They hadn't traveled to Mars.

They'd never left Earth.

Or maybe...

They had gone far, far beyond it.

They were gone.

One blink ago, Lar had his hand on Grace's shoulder, and Lisa was pressing her bloodied palm against the control panel, muttering about shutdown protocols. Now... nothing. No trace. No sound.

Jonas pressed his ear to the wall where Lisa had stood, his breathing harsh and uneven. It was still warm. Still beating.

"Do you hear that?" Grace whispered.

Jonas strained. At first, nothing. Then—scraping. Faint. Metal against stone. A single scream, stifled like it had been wrapped in a throat that refused to open fully.

He pulled back, jaw clenched. "They're not dead."

"How do you know?"

"Because whatever's doing this... it's not done playing."

The room flickered again — only this time, the countdown did not return. Instead, a single screen powered on, showing a hallway they recognized: the comms wing, Level C.

And Lar. Alone.

Running.

Bleeding.

The camera feed jittered. The walls twisted around him as he turned into a corridor that didn't exist. A sound followed him — something not human, wet and crawling. The camera cut out just before a hand — pale, stretched, jointed wrong — reached into frame from the ceiling vent.

"Wait," Grace breathed. "That's live. That's now."

Jonas's voice hardened. "We're going to find him."

He turned to Grace. "But if Lisa was taken too..."

A horrible thought surfaced in both their minds at once.

What if Lisa never left that room?

What if what disappeared with her... wasn't her?

They ran.

th the Vents

The tunnels beneath Level C weren't meant to be accessed—not by the crew. The maintenance ducts twisted through the station like arteries, narrow and hot, filled with dust and the occasional scrap of forgotten tools. But Jonas and Grace had no choice. The screen had shown Lar turning into one of these impossible paths. If he was still alive, he was down here.

Jonas led the way, crawling forward with a headlamp clamped to his forehead. His breathing echoed unnaturally off the metal, coming back distorted—like something was breathing back.

Behind him, Grace whispered, "Do you feel that?"

He stopped.

The metal under his palms was wet.

No leak. No condensation. Just... warm moisture, smeared across the steel like sweat.

The smell hit them both at once: salt, blood, rot.

Something had been dragged through here.

Far ahead, a rhythmic sound echoed. Not footsteps. Something softer. Faster.

Tapping.

Grace caught it too and tensed. "That's... fingers."

They rounded a bend.

The duct opened into a vertical shaft—and at the bottom, barely lit by a flashing hazard strobe, was a figure. Back turned. Arms twitching. Tapping.

Grace reached for her comm. "Lar?"

The figure twisted toward them with a sharp snap of the neck—but it wasn't Lar.

It wore his clothes.

Its face looked sewn into his skin.

Eyes wide, but the whites had been scribbled over in black marker. Mouth opened in a perpetual scream, lips stitched loosely together by what looked like stripped wire.

Grace screamed. Jonas pulled her back—but the creature didn't move. It just watched.

Then, from the vent above them, came a whisper—not over comms. Directly in their ears.

"One of you did this."

Jonas looked at Grace.

Grace looked at Jonas.

Neither spoke.

They climbed down anyway.

The shaft opened into a second room. One not on any schematic. A lab. Or a morgue. Or both.

Seventeen chairs. All positioned in a circle. At the center, a surgical table soaked in dry blood, rusted instruments scattered around it. Monitors lined the ceiling, each showing one of them—past and present. Footage from before the mission. Before the launch. Before the training.

Birthdays. Childhood.

Moments they never remembered.

Grace approached one screen.

It showed her as a child, sobbing in a hospital room.

"What is this?" she whispered.

Jonas didn't answer. He was frozen in front of another screen—his own. It showed him, no older than twelve, standing motionless in front of a mirror. A woman stood behind him, hand on his shoulder. Her mouth moved.

Jonas said nothing.

The screen glitched, looping the same frame: the woman whispering, Jonas not blinking.

Grace turned to him.

"Jonas... What is this place?"

He took a step backward.

The walls lit up—revealing writing etched into the metal. Symbols, repeated phrases in a looping spiral.

THEY ALL AGREED THEY ALL FORGOT THEY WERE MADE TO FORGET

Jonas clutched his head. "Something's wrong—this isn't the mission—this was never the mission—"

The lights blew out.

A deep voice echoed from inside the vents.

"Six left."

They turned.
Lar stood in the doorway.
Covered in blood.
Breathing hard.
"Lisa's dead," he said. "But she didn't die like the others. She... laughed. Right before it happened. Laughed like she remembered something we don't."

Jonas stepped forward. "What did she remember?"

Lar looked at him. "That we came here to kill each other."

They gathered in what remained of the habitat core—six figures huddled in a room too quiet, too still. The flickering overhead lights barely illuminated their faces, worn thin by weeks of grief, terror, and betrayal.

Jonas sat beside Grace, who hadn't spoken since they climbed out of the hidden shaft. Her hands were shaking, her eyes distant—watching that screen over and over again in her mind. The footage of herself as a child. The pain she didn't remember. The voice she somehow recognized.

Lar stood at the edge of the room, stained with blood that wasn't his. Lisa's blood. He wouldn't talk about what happened to her. He just said one thing, again and again:

"She laughed before she died."

Olivia sat across from him, body coiled tight. Her eyes flicked to the others, stopping longest on Elias—who had only recently reappeared and still refused to explain where he'd been. He stood silently, his face unreadable.

Renna, now visibly injured, leaned against the far wall, her breathing shallow. The wound on her leg had grown septic. She didn't complain, didn't ask for help. She just watched them all, fingers clenched tight around the bloody sample tube she hadn't let go of since the last murder.

Six left.

Six strangers.

None of them knew what was real anymore.

"Something's wrong with our memories," Olivia whispered. "I don't remember Lisa ever mentioning siblings. But in that footage from the room... she talked about her sister. For five minutes. In detail. I swear to you, I never heard her mention family before that."

Grace blinked slowly. "Jonas was in the footage too. As a child. But his eyes were different. Empty. Like someone had turned him off."

Jonas didn't respond. He was too busy tracing the line of the writing he'd copied from the secret room:

They all agreed.

They were made to forget.

The silence stretched. Then Elias spoke—calm, cold, almost detached.

"What if that room wasn't showing us memories?"

They turned to him.

"What if it was showing... conditioning?"

Grace paled.

Elias continued, walking slowly into the center of the group. "There are too many inconsistencies in how we remember things. Gaps. Flashbacks. None of us can agree on basic mission details anymore. What if... someone prepared us for something else before we ever left Earth?"

Lar stepped forward. "Like what?"

Elias looked directly at him.

"What if we were never meant to colonize Mars?"

"What if each of us was programmed... to kill one person?"

A silence fell like a guillotine.

Renna choked on her breath. "That's... that's insane."

Olivia whispered, "But what if he's right?"

"Then the killer is all of us."

The room darkened again as the emergency power flickered. Somewhere above them, a loud crash echoed through the station. Something heavy. Metal scraping metal.

Then—

Laughter.

Distorted.

Childlike.

From the vents.

The laughter of Lisa.

Dead Lisa.

The station's exterior door had been left slightly ajar. That was the first clue.

Jonas and Lar found it during a check of the secondary airlocks. The red lights along the perimeter blinked erratically—normally a warning for air-pressure instability, but now it pulsed like a heartbeat, irregular and panicked.

The door itself hadn't been forced. No sign of tampering.

Just open.

Widened enough for someone to slip through.

Or be dragged.

"Where's Renna?" Jonas asked, breath catching.

Lar turned pale. "She was just with us. In the main bay."

They looked at each other—and ran.

The trail of blood began just outside the bay. It wasn't a trail so much as drops, spaced in precise intervals, leading toward the old hydroponics wing. A place long abandoned after a radiation leak had corrupted the soil systems. No one had entered it in weeks.

The lights inside the wing had long died, leaving only the sharp beam of Jonas's flashlight cutting through the blackness.

And the walls—

God, the walls were covered.

Not in blood.

In symbols.

Painted in the same dried red Renna had used to mark her DNA samples. But these weren't notes or numbers. They were spirals. Phrases. Scratches. Over and over:

I REMEMBER NOW I REMEMBER NOW I REMEMBER NOW I REMEMBER—

Grace and Olivia caught up just as Jonas reached the greenhouse's central tank.

What remained of Renna was inside.

Folded.

Her body had been bent in on itself—every joint reversed—stuffed into the broken nutrient tank like meat into a jar. Her eyes had been removed, replaced with tiny glass vials filled with blood. Her mouth hung open, her tongue missing.

On her chest, carved in with surgical precision:

"WHO MADE YOU?"

Grace staggered back, hand clamped to her mouth.

Olivia dropped to her knees, the air punched out of her.

Lar stared blankly, then whispered, "No human could do that."

And yet... someone had.

Jonas looked up at the ceiling.

The glass above the greenhouse was shattered slightly. Mars' faint light—filtered through dust and storm—cast the scene in a sickly orange.

But in the reflection, just for a moment, Jonas thought he saw a figure watching them. Standing impossibly still. A silhouette behind the glass, unmoving.

Then gone.

"Was she the last?" Grace whispered.

"No," Jonas said quietly, breath trembling. "There are five of us left."

A pause.

Then Elias's voice crackled through the comms:

"No. There are four."

Static.

"I think I killed someone."

Silence.

Then—

"But I don't know who."

It was quiet in the base now. Too quiet.

The kind of silence that feels unnatural, as if the walls themselves were holding their breath.

Four of them remained: Jonas, Grace, Lar, and Olivia. Elias had vanished again after his cryptic comm message.

And Renna's horrific death still hung in the air like rot in the vents.

They no longer slept at night. Not truly.

Instead, they watched each other. Watched shadows. Watched the rooms. And deep down, each was beginning to wonder if it was already too late.

Jonas sat in the medical wing beside Grace, who was methodically sewing a long tear in her own jacket. A futile task, but she needed the repetition. He could see the tremor in her fingers.

"We're missing something," Jonas said quietly.

Grace didn't look up.

"Something bigger than one killer," he continued. "I think this all began before we landed. Maybe before we even trained."

Grace paused in her stitching. "Like programming?"

He nodded. "Like someone built this into us. Buried it deep."

She looked up then, eyes meeting his. "Why us?"

He didn't have an answer.

Olivia was alone in the data chamber.

Watching footage.

Again and again.

Her own face. Laughing.

Her own hands. Holding a knife.

A blurred body on the ground.

The footage skipped—glitched—and then she was gone from the screen, replaced by a new recording.

This time, Lar.

Standing over a bed.

The shape in the bed barely visible. Just a breathing lump.

And then Lar leaned forward, whispered something into the sleeper's ear.

The footage fuzzed.

And the body stopped breathing.

Olivia rewound. Again. And again.

No sound.

No expression.

Just murder in silence.

But the footage had no timestamp. No logs. No confirmation if it was real. Just like all the others.

She slammed the monitor off.

"We're being shown things to break us," she whispered.

"Or to remind us."

Lar was in the cargo wing.

He'd found something. A wall panel slightly misaligned. He unscrewed it slowly, hands steady despite his heartbeat rattling inside his skull.

Behind the panel—hidden in the insulation—was a case.

And in it:

A folder labeled CANDIDATES.

Profiles.

His face. Jonas's. Grace's. Olivia's.

Medical notes.

Psychological thresholds.

Conditioning schedules.

And at the bottom:

"One task. One target. One mission."

Lar's breath caught.

He closed the folder and whispered to no one, "They made us do this."

And behind him, in the dark of the corridor—a reflection moved.

Not his.

Not human.

The footage came without warning.

No logs. No alerts. It simply began to play on the central screen in the command module, just after midnight cycle.

Grace had been half-asleep on the floor, curled up beside the vent shaft where she'd taken to resting—closer to Jonas, when he stayed in the room. Lar had just finished patching one of the backup generators. Olivia was in the corner, staring into a mug of rehydrated coffee that had long gone cold.

And then the screen lit up.

The image was grainy, black and white — flickering with static like it had been tampered with or distorted by interference. But the shapes were unmistakable.

The corridor outside the hydroponics wing.

Renna.

And behind her — Jonas.

It wasn't like the other videos. This wasn't just a suggestion. There was no ambiguity.

It showed Jonas stepping forward, reaching for her. His expression is unreadable. His movements are too calm.

She turned, surprised.

He raised something — a scalpel. No hesitation. A single flash of motion.

Then it cut to static.

No sound.

Just proof.

Grace stood frozen, heart pounding so loudly she couldn't hear the others at first.

"No," she whispered. "No, that's not right."

"He did it," Olivia muttered. "That's... he murdered her."

Lar watched in silence. His mouth was tight, his hands clenched.

Grace shook her head. "This could be fabricated. We've seen manipulated footage before. Remember the looped feeds, the glitches—"

"But this one was real," Olivia snapped. "And you know it."

They confronted him within the hour.

Jonas had been in the lower maintenance hallway, trying to isolate a series of strange power surges in the system — the same ones he now suspected were tied to the hallucinations and electrical manipulations that had plagued them. He looked exhausted. His eyes sunken, skin pale. He looked... frightened.

But when Grace told him what they saw, he didn't deny it.

"I don't remember doing that," Jonas said, barely audible. "I swear to you, Grace... I don't remember anything like that."

His voice cracked on her name.

Lar stood to his side, stone-faced. "Maybe that's the point."

Jonas stepped back. "You really believe I did it?"

"I believe what we saw," Olivia said. "You don't remember, but that doesn't change what happened."

Grace hesitated. She could still feel the pressure of Jonas's hand from the last time he held hers. The look he gave her when he told her she made things feel sane, even for a moment.

"You're not giving me a chance," Jonas said, looking only at her.

"We're giving you a chance," Lar said. "To leave. Now."

They gave him a suit, minimal oxygen, and watched as he was sealed in the decompression chamber. Grace couldn't look away. She couldn't speak. Jonas stood behind the glass, looking at her with that calm sadness that she would never forget.

"Don't let them change you," he mouthed silently. "Not like they did me."

Then the outer doors opened.

He stepped into the red snow.

And then — the suit failed.

They didn't know why. A defect? A cut? Sabotage?

But it didn't matter. The pressure was too much.

Blood vessels burst in his eyes. His helmet cracked. His body spasmed — collapsed into the dirt with a silent, terrible grace.

Grace screamed.

She slammed her fists against the inner window, sobbing, as Olivia turned away, unable to stomach it. Lar simply stared, jaw clenched so hard his teeth ached.

The air inside the base felt colder now.

As if Jonas had taken the last of the warmth with him.

Grace didn't speak for hours.

After Jonas died in the dust, after his body stopped twitching and froze where it fell, she sat in the med bay—alone. Not tending to wounds, not sorting inventory. Just... sitting.

The overhead lights flickered in an off-rhythm stutter, casting faint shadows that reached toward her, then vanished. She didn't blink. She didn't move. She just stared at the spot on the floor where he used to leave his boots.

It had been his corner. He always took the corner. "So I can see everything," he once said.

Now there was nothing to see.

The rest of the crew stayed away from her. Olivia was buried in system logs and scans again, muttering to herself. Lar occasionally passed by the bay's door, but never entered. Maybe he didn't know what to say. Maybe he thought she'd be next.

Grace remembered the way Jonas looked before the outer doors opened — the sorrow in his eyes, the resignation. Not rage. Not guilt. Just... heartbreak. And then the way he mouthed those final words:

"Don't let them change you."

A soft sob broke through her lips before she could stop it.

Grace buried her face in her hands, and for the first time since they arrived on this cursed rock, she wept uncontrollably. Not the silent, restrained tears of someone afraid to be heard. These were broken sounds — grief in its rawest form.

She cried until her breath hitched.

Until the sobs turned into a dry, shaking silence.

She hadn't slept.

Couldn't.

Instead, she went back to the footage. The one that condemned Jonas.

She stared at every frame.

She paused it. Rewound. Zoomed.

And then something shifted.

In the corner — barely visible in the static — she saw it. A flicker. A ghosting effect. A double outline around Jonas's body, like a layering error in a 3D render. Like someone added him into the footage.

Her heart dropped.

"No..."

She checked the timestamp metadata. It was erased. That was strange enough.

But more than that—she realized this recording hadn't come through the primary surveillance system at all.

It had been injected.

Her fingers trembled.

She could barely breathe. If that was true...

Jonas didn't do it.

He died for nothing.

Grace staggered back from the terminal. Her body felt like it was folding in on itself.

"Jonas..." she whispered. Her voice cracked like brittle ice.

Then came the rage.

She ripped the chair from its bolts and threw it across the room. Glass shattered. Monitors sparked.

"WHO'S DOING THIS?!"

She screamed at the walls, at the cameras, at the Godless void that had swallowed the people she cared about one by one. Her voice echoed in the vents. No answer.

No answer.

She found herself in the comms wing a few hours later, staring at the dark screen, wondering if she should call Earth.

But would Earth even answer?

Would it even matter?

What if they were behind this?

What if they'd always been?

She returned to the med bay eventually.

Sat again. In silence.

Looked at Jonas's old jacket, still hanging from the hook.

She reached out, gently, and pressed her hand to it.

It was cold.

She imagined his hand over hers, warm like it used to be.

She imagined him whispering to her: Keep going. Find the truth. Don't let them win.

In the dark, Grace swore something moved past the window.

A flicker of shadow.

A whisper that didn't belong to memory.

She sat still.

Eyes narrowed.

And this time, she didn't cry.

She listened.

And she prepared.

Because Jonas may be dead.

But whoever did this?

They were still inside.

CHAPTER XV

Red dust

It began with a scream — distant, muffled, yet unmistakable. Grace snapped upright from her shallow sleep in the medbay, heart slamming against her chest. The lights flickered, and the hum of the base systems sounded... off. Slower. As if the station itself were holding its breath.

Olivia was already running by the time Grace reached the corridor. Lisa followed behind, holding a rifle that rattled in her shaking hands. "Something's wrong," Lisa muttered, more to herself than anyone else. "I checked the outer doors last night... one was slightly open. Just slightly."

In the observation chamber, Jonas stood alone, staring at a blood smear across the glass. It was wide, dragging from ceiling to floor — as though someone had been pulled up and out. But no body remained. Just the red. And a small strip of flesh.

"Where's Lar?" Olivia demanded.

Jonas turned slowly. "I don't know. But something's happening. I think... someone's hiding something."

Olivia stepped closer. "Who?"

Jonas swallowed. "I think it's me."

The room fell into silence. Everyone stared at him.

"I don't remember the last few hours. I blacked out... and when I came to, there was blood on my boots."

Lisa lifted the gun slightly. "You think you did this?"

"I don't know, Lisa. That's the worst part. I don't know anything anymore."

Then, Grace noticed something flickering on the terminal. A new log — dated minutes ago.

Audio file: 03:19:27

The voice was distorted. But not unfamiliar.

"They're starting to doubt. Good. It'll be easier once they turn on each other. I've adapted. They'll never know who it is. The body is just a shell... they'll never see what's beneath."

The voice was Lar's.

The room was thrown into chaos. Olivia ran to the systems panel, trying to trace the log's source. Lisa cursed loudly, backing away, gun shaking. "That's not possible—he's one of us! He's been with us since day one!"

"Exactly," Grace said coldly. "And we never questioned who he was before that."

They split into two teams — Grace and Jonas to track Lar's location via biosignals, and Olivia and Lisa to search the central corridor. As Grace moved through the flickering sublevel, she heard it. A noise too unnatural to be footsteps. Wet. Slithering. Something alive.

She turned a corner and stopped.

There was a smear of blood leading to a sealed hatch labeled "Maintenance 07 – Access Restricted". The maintenance sector hadn't been used since arrival.

But now... someone was in there.

Jonas touched the keypad. "It's not locked anymore."

The hatch opened.

Inside was a room none of them had ever seen on the blueprint. It wasn't a supply closet or control room.

It was surgical. A circular operating table. Restraints. Tools far too advanced for their expedition. And a series of containment tanks... all empty.

Grace stepped forward, her voice barely audible: "This... this is where they made him."

The terminal buzzed. Another file blinked onto the screen:

SUBJECT: LAR — Status: Stable Integration. Host no longer aware of previous form. Continue surveillance. Trigger at Phase Omega.

Jonas looked at Grace, horror on his face. "He's not human. He was never human."

Suddenly, behind them, a voice.

"I never lied," Lar whispered.

The door slammed shut.

And the screaming began.

The silence was no longer silence. It breathed.

It came from under the floor, pulsing through the steel panels like a slow heartbeat. Olivia stood near the main terminal, her hand hovering above the emergency comms panel, her other clutching a bloody wrench. The comms were still dead. A static that once felt technical... now felt sentient. Watching. Listening.

Grace was the first to speak. "We're not alone here."

Her voice didn't tremble. But her eyes did — flicking from face to face in the command room. Lisa stood by the door, blaster trembling in her grip. Two others were missing already — Renna and Elias — vanished without a trace. Or so they thought.

Until the screaming started.

The sound came from behind the ventilation shaft — not mechanical, not even human. It was a wet sound. Bones against steel. A dragging sound that twisted Olivia's stomach. She turned — just as blood began to pool from the vents overhead.

Lisa screamed and stepped back. Something thudded. A piece of a jaw. Torn clean. Still twitching.

"What the hell is happening!?" Olivia gasped, backing away.

Grace knelt, her gloved hands over the red pool. She whispered, "This isn't like the others. This... this is surgical."

Then Jonas stumbled in.

His suit was torn, his left arm broken, limp and hanging by a thread of tendon and sleeve. He fell forward, blood blooming beneath him. But it wasn't his injuries that made Grace reel back in horror. It was what he said:

"Lar. It's Lar. He's not—he's not one of us—he never was—"

And then he collapsed, unconscious.

Silence returned. And then... from the far hallway — footsteps. Slow. Purposeful.

The hallway lights began to flicker.

They gathered Jonas in the infirmary, Grace working to stabilize him, while Olivia stared at the monitor. Footage. Something had finally been recorded.

A grainy, flickering video from an external rover camera. It showed Lar... standing still outside the western dome — his eyes completely black, his skin rippling, moving as if something beneath it wanted out.

Lisa's breath caught. "What... is he?"

No one spoke. No one could.

Until Olivia clicked on the next file. A log file.

PROJECT VERMIS

Specimen 01 status: Host integration successful. Psychological adaptation complete. Subject unaware of its origin. Observation continues.

"This... this isn't us," Grace whispered. "This wasn't part of the mission."

A loud clang rang from the air duct above.

Then they heard it — the whisper. Not in their ears. In their minds. A voice like cracking bone, like rotting wind:

"You were never meant to leave."

They split up. Stupid. Desperate.

Grace dragged Jonas toward the emergency shuttle dock. Olivia and Lisa armed themselves, moving through the base with weapons raised, following the blood trail that led deeper — into the sublevels, where the lights hadn't worked in weeks.

They found Renna. Or what was left of her.

Hung upside down. Limbs rearranged like a grotesque sculpture. Her eyes were still blinking — removed from her head and pinned to the wall like trophies.

Lisa vomited. Olivia screamed.

And then the lights all died.

In the pitch black, something breathed behind them.

A shape lunged.

Lisa's scream was cut off with a sickening crunch.

Back at the shuttle dock, Grace had managed to get Jonas inside. The engines hummed to life. But as she sealed the hatch, she saw him.

Lar.

Not walking. Floating in the corridor.

His body cracked open like an egg — skin peeling, bones shifting, face elongating into something alien and wrong. His eyes were endless voids, and his mouth stretched across his face, jagged and too wide.

He looked at her. And smiled.

The screaming cut through the steel corridors like a siren from hell.

Lisa and Olivia sprinted toward the hatch, following the echo of Grace's voice — but as they reached Maintenance 07, the panel was scorched and melted, as if clawed by something far stronger than human hands. Jonas was inside. So was Grace. And Lar.

"Override it!" Olivia shouted, fumbling at the manual lock. Lisa dropped to her knees, pulling open the emergency fuse panel, sparks catching her gloves. The hum of something massive stirred within the sealed room beyond.

Then — silence.

The door slid open.

Jonas stumbled out, blood soaking his face and shirt. Grace followed seconds later, eyes wide, her hands trembling. Inside, the surgical room was empty. Except for the thing curled in the corner. It looked almost like Lar. Almost.

But what crouched there had no eyes — only slits of thin silver. Its mouth ran vertically down the center of its head, pulsing, split into two jagged flaps like a torn muscle. And its limbs — elongated, spiderlike, coated in strands of dried skin and blood — flexed slowly, as if it were trying to remember how to wear the human form again.

"He's not dead," Grace whispered. "He let us go."

"Why?" Lisa asked.

Jonas turned to her, jaw clenched. "Because he wants us to run. It's a hunt now."

They regrouped in the central command hall. Renna and Elias had vanished — their rooms empty, bunks soaked in blackened blood. Footage was gone. Wiped. The logs had rewritten themselves to show only static. Lar had taken control of the base systems.

"We're rats in a cage," Olivia said, pacing. "Everything we thought was broken — the comms, the power failures, the blackouts — it wasn't sabotage. It was controlled. Psychological conditioning. We've been watching from the start."

Lisa turned sharply to Jonas. "What was he doing in that lab? Did you see what was on the screens?"

Jonas nodded slowly. "Experiments. On us. On others before us. It wasn't just surveillance... It was learning how to be human."

Grace sat in the corner, hands clenched, trying to calm her shaking breaths. "He's not like anything I've seen. Not alien in a traditional sense. It's like... like something ancient. Biological horror. A mimic with a purpose we can't comprehend."

And then came the footage.

A screen flickered alive.

It showed Renna — walking alone down the hydroponics corridor. A slow, uneasy walk. Behind her, a shadow peeled off the wall. The footage warped and distorted — frame by frame — as something moved within the pixels. Lar. In-between. Not man. Not monster.

A click.

The screen went black.

When they reached hydroponics, they found Renna's hand. Just her hand. Still clutching her scanner, frozen mid-record.

No blood. No body. Just the sound of fluid dripping — from the vent above.

Jonas looked up, flashlight trembling.

Two feet dangled.

The rest of her was jammed inside the duct, bones cracking where they shouldn't bend.

Lisa collapsed. Olivia backed away, hands to her mouth.

Grace stepped forward — numb, distant, staring not at Renna... but the wall behind her. In dried blood, scrawled in something not quite human handwriting:

"YOU ARE THE VIRUS. I AM THE CURE."

The atmosphere turned electric. Paranoia festered like rot. No one trusted the other. Olivia began checking weapons, rationing air tanks. Jonas disappeared into the eastern tunnels for hours. Grace stopped sleeping.

Then Elias returned.

He wandered into the medbay half-naked, eyes blackened, skin peeled at the edges like it was trying to slough off.

He didn't speak.

He simply collapsed at Grace's feet, whispering:

"He's wearing their faces now."

Not with flames — but with chaos. Panels flickered. Doors slammed shut without warning. The air scrubbers choked. It was as if the very structure was suffocating, alive, turning against what was left of the crew.

Grace stumbled through the hallway, supporting Olivia, who was bleeding badly from her side. Lisa was behind them, limping, carrying the last oxygen tank. Jonas was gone. Taken. Ripped apart in front of their eyes as Lar — no longer pretending to be human — unfurled from the dark like something born from the void.

His skin had split open in jagged ridges, revealing layers of bone, sinew, and something slick and glowing beneath — an intelligence that didn't belong to Earth or anything known to it. Lar had spoken only once before the massacre began:

"You were never chosen. You were sent. Like bait. And now the hunt ends."

They had seen what was beneath his skin — rows of hollow eyes, twitching tendrils that sensed movement like sonar. He had discarded his voice. His words now came in pulses — waves in their minds, sickening, warm, intimate.

Grace had managed to escape with Olivia and Lisa, just barely, ducking into the emergency tunnels beneath Engineering. They reached the hangar — the last escape pod still intact. The rest were gone, ripped apart or buried under rubble.

Lisa shoved open the pod hatch and began loading emergency supplies.

Olivia leaned against the metal, whispering deliriously. "He watched us... all this time. Not just from the walls. From inside. I heard him in my dreams. Jonas knew. He always knew."

Grace turned to her — but Olivia's eyes were glassy. A long, thin gash opened down her throat as she slid to the ground. The blood pooled like ink.

Behind her stood Lar.

No longer a man. No longer needing disguise.

He was tall — stretched unnaturally, wearing scraps of skin like trophies. His hands were long, multi-jointed, and his face... had none of the humanity he once wore.

Lisa screamed and raised her weapon — but Lar didn't move. He only stared at Grace. Not through her, but into her. As if memorizing her.

And then... he stepped back.

He let her go.

The pod hissed shut just as Lisa hit the launch.

The force slammed Grace against the wall. Lisa was gone. The hatch had crushed her leg. She had bled out during ascent. Grace screamed, alone, bathed in red light from Mars below as the pod tore into the sky.

Through the window, she saw him.

Lar. Standing outside the hangar. Watching. His form twitching, folding into itself. He had let her live.

Not out of mercy.

But to send a message.

Grace wept — not for the dead — but because she realized: this was never about killing them all.

It was about letting one survive.

To carry the fear back to Earth.

The Author

DHRUV TRIPATHI

www.ingramcontent.com/pod-product-compliance
Lightning Source LLC
Chambersburg PA
CBHW031149160726
47991CB00004B/1599